The Collected Supernatural and Weird Fiction of Harriet Beecher Stowe

The Collected Supernatural and Weird Fiction of Harriet Beecher Stowe

Eight Short Stories of the Strange and Unusual Including 'The Ghost in the Mill,' 'How to Fight the Devil' and 'The Visit to the Haunted House'

Harriet Beecher Stowe

LEONAUR

The Collected
Supernatural and Weird
Fiction of
Harriet Beecher Stowe
Eight Short Stories of the Strange and Unusual Including 'The Ghost in the Mill,'
'How to Fight the Devil' and 'The Visit to the Haunted House'

by Harriet Beecher Stowe

Leonaur is an imprint of Oakpast Ltd

Copyright in this form © 2021 Oakpast Ltd

ISBN: 978-1-78282-976-8 (hardcover)
ISBN: 978-1-78282-977-5 (softcover)

http://www.leonaur.com

Publisher's Notes

The views expressed in this book are not necessarily
those of the publisher.

Contents

The Ghost in the Mill

"Come, Sam, tell us a story," said I, as Harry and I crept to his knees, in the glow of the bright evening firelight; while Aunt Lois was busily rattling the tea-things, and grandmamma, at the other end of the fireplace, was quietly setting the heel of a blue-mixed yarn stocking.

In those days we had no magazines and daily papers, each reeling off a serial story. Once a week, *The Columbian Sentinel* came from Boston with its slender stock of news and editorial; but all the multiform devices—pictorial, narrative, and poetical—which keep the mind of the present generation ablaze with excitement, had not then even an existence. There was no theatre, no opera; there were in Oldtown no parties or balls, except, perhaps, the annual election, or Thanksgiving festival; and when winter came, and the sun went down at half-past four o'clock, and left the long, dark hours of evening to be provided for, the necessity of amusement became urgent.

Hence, in those days, chimney-corner story-telling became an art and an accomplishment. Society then was full of traditions and narratives which had all the uncertain glow and shifting mystery of the firelit hearth upon them. They were told to sympathetic audiences, by the rising and falling light of the solemn embers, with the hearth-crickets filling up every pause. Then the aged told their stories to the young—tales of early life; tales of war and adventure, of forest-days, of Indian captivities and escapes, of bears and wild-cats and panthers, of rattlesnakes, of witches and wizards, and strange and wonderful dreams and

7

SAM LAWSON.

appearances and providences.

In those days of early Massachusetts, faith and credence were in the very air. Two-thirds of New England was then dark, unbroken forests, through whose tangled paths the mysterious winter wind groaned and shrieked and howled with weird noises and unaccountable clamours. Along the iron-bound shore, the stormful Atlantic raved and thundered, and dashed its moaning waters, as if to deaden and deafen any voice that might tell of the settled life of the old civilized world, and shut us forever into the wilderness. A good story-teller, in those days, was always sure of a warm seat at the hearthstone, and the delighted homage of children; and in all Oldtown there was no better story-teller than Sam Lawson.

"Do, do, tell us a story," said Harry, pressing upon him, and opening very wide blue eyes, in which undoubting faith shone as in a mirror; "and let it be something strange, and different from common."

"Wal, I know lots o' strange things," said Sam, looking mysteriously into the fire. "Why, I know things, that ef I should tell—why, people might say they wa'n't so; but then they is so for all that."

"Oh, *do*, do, tell us!"

"Why, I should scare ye to death, mebbe," said Sam doubtingly.

"Oh, pooh! no, you wouldn't," we both burst out at once.

But Sam was possessed by a reticent spirit, and loved dearly to be wooed and importuned; and so, he only took up the great kitchen-tongs, and smote on the hickory forestick, when it flew apart in the middle, and scattered a shower of clear bright coals all over the hearth.

"Mercy on us, Sam Lawson!" said Aunt Lois in an indignant voice, spinning round from her dishwashing.

"Don't you worry a grain, Miss Lois," said Sam composedly. "I see that 'are stick was e'en a'most in two, and I thought I'd jest settle it. I'll sweep up the coals now," he added, vigorously applying a turkey-wing to the purpose, as he knelt on the

"*Do, do, tell us a story.*"

hearth, his spare, lean figure glowing in the blaze of the firelight, and getting quite flushed with exertion.

"There, now!" he said, when he had brushed over and under and between the fire-irons, and pursued the retreating ashes so far into the red, fiery citadel, that his finger-ends were burning and tingling, "that are's done now as well as Hepsy herself could 'a' done it. I allers sweeps up the haarth: I think it's part o' the man's bisness when he makes the fire. But Hepsy's so used to seein' me a-doin' on't, that she don't see no kind o' merit in't. It's just as Parson Lothrop said in his sermon—folks allers overlook their common marcies"—

"But come, Sam, that story," said Harry and I coaxingly, pressing upon him, and pulling him down into his seat in the corner.

"Lordy massy, these 'ere young uns!" said Sam. "There's never no contentin' on 'em: ye tell 'em one story, and they jest swallows it as a dog does a gob o' meat; and they're all ready for another. What do ye want to hear now?"

Now, the fact was, that Sam's stories had been told us so often, that they were all arranged and ticketed in our minds. We knew every word in them, and could set him right if he varied a hair from the usual track; and still the interest in them was un abated. Still we shivered, and clung to his knee, at the mysterious parts, and felt gentle, cold chills run down our spines at appropriate places. We were always in the most receptive and sympathetic condition.

Tonight, in particular, was one of chose thundering stormy ones, when the winds appeared to be holding a perfect mad carnival over my grandfather's house. They yelled and squealed round the corners; they collected in troops, and came tumbling and roaring down chimney; they shook and rattled the buttery-door and the sinkroom-door and the cellar-door and the chamber-door, with a constant undertone of squeak and clatter, as if at every door were a cold, discontented spirit, tired of the chill outside, and longing for the warmth and comfort within.

"Wal, boys," said Sam confidentially, "what'll ye have?"

"Tell us *Come down, come down!*" we both shouted with one

voice. This was, in our mind, an "A No. 1" among Sam's stories.

"Ye mus'n't be frightened now," said Sam paternally.

"Oh, no! we ar'n't frightened ever" said we both in one breath.

"Not when ye go down the cellar arter cider?" said Sam with severe scrutiny. "Ef ye should be down cellar, and the candle should go out, now?"

"I ain't," said I: "I ain't afraid of anything. I never knew what it was to be afraid in my life."

"Wal, then," said Sam, "I'll tell ye. This 'ere's what Cap'n Eb Sawin told me when I was a boy about your bigness, I reckon.

"Cap'n Eb Sawin was a most respectable man. Your gran'ther knew him very well; and he was a deacon in the church in Dedham afore he died. He was at Lexington when the fust gun was fired agin the British. He was a dreffle smart man, Cap'n Eb was, and driv team a good many years atween here and Boston. He married Lois Peabody, that was cousin to your gran'ther then. Lois was a rael sensible woman; and I've heard her tell the story as he told her, and it was jest as he told it to me—jest exactly; and I shall never forget it if I live to be nine hundred years old, like Mathuselah.

"Ye see, along back in them times, there used to be a fellow come round these 'ere parts, spring and fall, a-peddlin' goods, with, his pack on his back; and his name was Jehigl Lommedieu. Nobody rightly knew where he come from. He wasn't much of a talker; but the women rather liked him, and kind o' liked to have him round. Women will like some fellows, when men can't see no sort o' reason why they should; and they liked this 'ere Lommedieu, though he was kind o' mournful and thin and shad-bellied, and hadn't nothin' to say for himself. But it got to be so, that the women would count and calculate so many weeks afore 'twas time for Lommedieu to be along; and they'd make up gingersnaps and preserves and pies, and make him stay to tea at the houses, and feed him up on the best there was: and the story went round, that he was a-courtin' Phebe Ann Parker, or Phebe Ann was a-courtin' him,—folks didn't rightly know which. Wal, all of a sudden, Lommedieu stopped comin' round; and nobody knew why—only jest he didn't come. It turned out that Phebe Ann Parker had got a letter from him, sayin' he'd be along afore Thanksgiving; but he didn't come, neither afore nor at Thanksgiving time, nor arter, nor next spring: and finally, the women they gin up lookin' for him. Some said he was dead; some said he was gone to Canada; and some said he hed gone over to the Old Country.

"Wal, as to Phebe Ann, she acted like a gal o' sense, and married 'Bijah Moss, and thought no more 'bout it. She took the right view on't, and said she was sartin that all things was ordered out for the best; and it was jest as well folks couldn't always have their own way. And so, in time, Lommedieu was gone out o' folks's minds, much as a last year's apple-blossom.

"It's relly affectin' to think how little these 'ere folks is missed that's so much sot by. There ain't nobody, ef they's ever so important, but what the world gets to goin' on without 'em, pretty much as it did with 'em, though there's some little flurry at fust. Wal, the last thing that was in anybody's mind was, that they ever should hear from Lommedieu agin. But there ain't nothin' but what has its time o' turnin' up; and it seems his turn was to come.

"Wal, ye see, 'twas the 19th o' March, when Cap'n Eb Sawin started with a team for Boston. That day, there come on about the biggest snowstorm that there'd been in them parts sence the Oldest man could remember. 'Twas this 'ere fine, siftin' snow, that drives in your face like needles, with a wind to cut your nose off: it made teamin' pretty tedious work. Cap'n Eb was about the toughest man in them parts. He'd spent days in the woods a-loggin', and he'd been up to the deestrict o' Maine a-lumberin', and was about up to any sort o' thing a man gen'ally could be up to; but these 'ere March winds sometimes does set on a fellow so, that neither natur' nor grace can stan' 'em. The cap'n used to say he could stan' any wind that blew one way't time for five minutes; but come to winds that blew all four p'ints at the same minit—why, they flustered him.

"Wal, that was the sort o' weather it was all day: and by sundown Cap'n Eb he got clean bewildered, so that he lost his road; and, when night came on, he didn't know nothin' where he was. Ye see the country was all under drift, and the air so thick with snow, that he couldn't see a foot afore him; and the fact was, he got off the Boston road without knowin' it, and came out at a pair o' bars nigh upon Sherburn, where old Cack Sparrock's mill is.

"Your gran'ther used to know old Cack, boys. He was a drefful drinkin' old crittur, that lived there all alone in the woods by himself a-tendin' saw and grist mill. He wa'n't allers jest what he was then. Time was that Cack was a pretty consid'ably likely young man, and his wife was a very respectable woman—Deacon Amos Petengall's dater from Sherburn.

"But ye see, the year arter his wife died, Cack he gin up goin' to meetin' Sundays, and, all the tithing-men and selectmen could do, they couldn't get him out to meetin'; and, when a man neglects means o' grace and sanctuary privileges, there ain't no sayin' what he'll do next. Why, boys, jist think on't!—an immortal crittur lyin' round loose all day Sunday, and not puttin' on so much as a clean shirt, when all 'spectable folks has on their best close, and is to meetin' worshippin' the Lord! What can you spect to come of it, when he lies idlin' round in his old week-day close, fishing, or some sich, but what the Devil should be arter him at last, as he was arter old Cack?"

Here Sam winked impressively to my grandfather in the opposite corner, to call his attention to the moral which he was interweaving with his narrative.

"Wal, ye see, Cap'n Eb he told me, that when he come to them bars and looked up, and saw the dark a-comin' down, and the storm a-thickenin' up, he felt that things was gettin' pretty consid'able serious There was a dark piece o' woods on ahead of him inside the bars; and he knew, come to get in there, the fight would give out clean. So, he jest thought he'd take the boss out o' the team, and go ahead a little, and see where he was. So, he driv his oxen up ag'in the fence, and took out the boss, and

14

got on him, and pushed along through the woods, not rightly knowin' where he was goin'.

"Wal, afore long he see a fight through the trees and, sure enough, he come out to Cack Sparrock's old mill.

"It was a pretty consid'able gloomy sort of a place, that 'are old mill was. There was a great fall of water that come rushin' down the rocks, and fell in a deep pool: and it sounded sort o' wild and lonesome: but Cap'n Eb he knocked on the door with his whip-handle, and got in.

"There, to be sure, sot old Cack beside a great blazin' fire, with his rum-jug at his elbow. He was a drefful fellow to drink, Cack was! For all that, there was some good in him, for he was pleasant-spoken and 'bliging; and he made the cap'n welcome.

"'Ye see, Cack,' said Cap'n Eb, 'I'm off my road, and got snowed up down by your bars,' says he.

"'Want ter know!' says Cack. 'Calculate you'll jest have to camp down here till mornin',' says he.

"Wal, so old Cack he got out his tin lantern, and went with Cap'n Eb back to the bars to help him fetch along his critturs. He told him he could put 'em under the mill-shed. So, they got the critturs up to the shed, and got the cart under; and by that time the storm was awful.

"But Cack he made a great roarin' fire, 'cause, ye see, Cack allers had slab-wood a plenty from his mill; and a roarin' fire is jest so much company. It sort o keeps a fellow's spirits up, a good fire does. So Cack he sot on his old teakettle, and made a swingeing lot o' toddy; and he and Cap'n Eb were havin' a tol'able comfortable time there. Cack was a pretty good hand to tell stories; and Cap'n Eb warn't no way backward in that line, and kep' up his end pretty well: and pretty soon they was a-roarin' and haw-hawin' inside about as loud as the storm outside; when all of a sudden, 'bout midnight, there come a loud rap on the door.

"'Lordy massy! what's that?' says Cack. Folks is rather startled allers to be checked up sudden when they are a-carryin' on and laughin'; and it was such an awful blowy night, it was a little scary to have a rap on the door.

"Wal, they waited a minit, and didn't hear nothin' but the wind a-screechin' round the chimbley; and old Cack was jest goin' on with his story, when the rap come ag'in, harder'n ever, as if it'd shook the door open.

"'Wal,' says old Cack, 'if 'tis the Devil, we'd jest as good's open, and have it out with him to onst,' says he; and so, he got up and opened the door, and, sure enough, there was old Ketury there. Expect you've heard your grandma tell about old Ketury. She used to come to meetin's sometimes, and her husband was one o' the prayin' Indians; but Ketury was one of the rael wild sort, and you couldn't no more convert *her* than you could convert a wild-cat or a painter (panther). Lordy massy! Ketury used to come to meetin', and sit there on them Indian benches; and when the second bell was a-tollin', and when Pason Lothrop and his wife was comin' up the broad aisle, and everybody in the house ris' up and stood, Ketury would sit there, and look at 'em out o' the corner o' her eyes; and folks used to say she rattled them necklaces o' rattlesnakes' tails and wild-cat teeth, and sich like heathen trumpery, and looked for all the world as if the spirit of the old Sarpent himself was in her.

"I've seen her sit and look at Lady Lothrop out o' the corner o' her eyes; and her old brown baggy neck would kind o' twist and work; and her eyes they looked so, that 'twas enough to scare a body. For all the world, she looked jest as if she was a-workin' up to spring at her. Lady Lothrop was jest as kind to Ketury as she always was to every poor crittur. She'd bow and smile as gracious to her when meetin was over, and she come down the aisle, passin' out o, meetin'; but Ketury never took no notice. Ye see, Ketury's father was one o' them great *powwows* down to Martha's Vineyard; and people used to say she was set apart, when she was a child, to the sarvice o' the Devil: any way, she never could be made nothin' of in a Christian way.

"She come down to Parson Lothrop's study once or twice to be *catechised*; but he couldn't get a word out o' her, and she kind o' seemed to sit scornful while he was a-talkin'. Folks said, if it was in old times, Ketury wouldn't have been allowed to

16

go on so; but Parson Lothrop's so sort o' mild, he let her take pretty much her own way. Everybody thought that Ketury was a witch: at least, she knew consid'able more'n she ought to know, and so they was kind o' 'fraid on her. Cap'n Eb says he never see a fellow seem scareder than Cack did when he see Ketury a-standin' there.

"Why, ye see, boys, she was as withered and wrinkled and brown as an old frosted punkin-vine; and her little snaky eyes sparkled and snapped, and it made yer head kind o' dizzy to look at 'em; and folks used to say that anybody that Ketury got mad at was sure to get the worst of it fust or last. And so, no matter what day or hour Ketury had a mind to rap at anybody's door, folks gen'lly thought it was best to let her in; but then, they never thought her coming was for any good, for she was just like the wind,—she came when the fit was on her, she staid jest so long as it pleased her, and went when she got ready, and not before. Ketury understood English, and could talk it well enough, but always seemed to scorn it, and was allers mowin' and mutterin' to herself in Indian, and winkin' and blinkin' as if she saw more folks round than you did, so that she wa'n't no way pleasant company; and yet everybody took good care to be polite to her.

"So old Cack asked her to come in, and didn't make no question where she come from, or what she come on; but he knew it was twelve good miles from where she lived to his hut, and the snow was drifted above her middle: and Cap'n Eb declared that there wa'n't no track, nor sign o' a track, of anybody's coming through that snow next morning."

"How did she get there, then?" said I.

"Didn't ye never see brown leaves a-ridin' on the wind? Well, Cap'n Eb he says, 'she came on the wind,' and I'm sure it was strong enough to fetch her. But Cack he got her down into the warm corner, and he poured her out a mug o' hot toddy, and give her: but ye see her bein' there sort o' stopped the conversation; for she sot there a-rockin' back'ards and for'ards, a-sippin her toddy, and a-mutterin', and lookin' up chimbley.

"Cap'n Eb says in all his born days he never hearn such

screeches and yells as the wind give over that chimbley; and old Cack got so frightened, you could fairly hear his teeth chatter.

"But Cap'n Eb he was a putty brave man, and he wa'n't goin' to have conversation stopped by no woman, witch or no witch; and so, when he see her mutterin', and lookin' up chimbley, he spoke up, and says he, 'Well, Ketury, what do you see?' says he. 'Come, out with it; don't keep it to yourself.' Ye see Cap'n Eb was a hearty fellow, and then he was a leetle warmed up with the toddy.

"Then he said he see an evil kind o' smile on Ketury's face, and she rattled her necklace o' bones and snakes' tails; and her eyes seemed to snap; and she looked up the chimbley, and called out, 'Come down, come down! let's see who ye be.'

"Then there was a scratchin' and a rumblin' and a groan; and a pair of feet come down the chimbley, and stood right in the middle of the haarth, the toes pi'ntin' out'rds, with shoes and silver buckles a-shin- in' in the firelight. Cap'n Eb says he never come so near bein' scared in his life; and, as to old Cack, he jest wilted right down in his chair.

"Then old Ketury got up, and reached her stick up chimbley, and called out louder, 'Come down, come down! let's see who ye be.' And, sure enough, down came a pair o' legs, and j'ined right on to the feet: good fair legs they was, with ribbed stockings and leather breeches.

"'Wal, we're in for it now,' says Cap'n Eb. 'Go it, Ketury, and let's have the rest on him.'

"Ketury didn't seem to mind him: she stood there as stiff as a stake, and kep' callin' out, 'Come down, come down! let's see who ye be.' And then come down the body of a man with a brown coat and yellow vest, and j'ined right on to the legs; but there wa'n't no arms to it. Then Ketury shook her stick up chimbley, and called, '*Come down, come down!*' And there came down a pair o' arms, and went on each side o' the body; and there stood a man all finished, only there wa'n't no head on him.

"'Wal, Ketury,' says Cap'n Eb, 'this 'ere's getting serious. I 'spec' you must finish him up, and let's see what he wants of us.'

"Then Ketury called out once more, louder'n ever, 'Come down, come down! let's see who ye be.' And, sure enough, down comes a man's head, and settled on the shoulders straight enough; and Cap'n Eb, the minit he sot eyes on him, knew he was Jehiel Lommedieu.

"Old Cack knew him too; and he fell flat on his face, and prayed the Lord to have mercy on his soul: but Cap'n Eb he was for gettin' to the bottom of matters, and not have his scare for nothin'; so he says to him, 'What do you want, now you hev come?'

"The man he didn't speak; he only sort o' moaned, and p'inted to the chimbley. He seemed to try to speak, but couldn't; for ye see it isn't often that his sort o' folks is permitted to speak: but just then there came a screechin' blast o' wind, and blowed the door open, and blowed the smoke and fire all out into the room, and there seemed to be a whirlwind and darkness and moans and screeches; and, when it all cleared up, Ketury and the man was both gone, and only old Cack lay on the ground, rolling and moaning as if he'd die.

"Wal, Cap'n Eb he picked him up, and built up the fire, and sort o' comforted him up, 'cause the crittur was in distress o' mind that was drefful. The awful Providence, ye see, had awakened him, and his sin had been set home to his soul; and he was under such conviction, that it all had to come out,—how old Cack's father had murdered poor Lommedieu for his money, and Cack had been privy to it, and helped his father build the body up in that very chimbley; and he said that he hadn't had neither peace nor rest since then, and that was what had driv' him away from ordinances; for ye know sinnin' will always make a man leave prayin'.

"Wal, Cack didn't live but a day or two. Cap'n Eb he got the minister o' Sherburn and one o' the selectmen down to see him; and they took his deposition. He seemed railly quite penitent; and Parson Carryl he prayed with him, and was faithful in settin' home the providence to his soul: and so, at the eleventh hour, poor old Cack might have got in; at least it looks a leetle like it.

" Old Cack knew him too."

He was distressed to think he couldn't live to be hung. He sort o' seemed to think, that if he was fairly tried, and hung, it would make it all square. He made Parson Carryl promise to have the old mill pulled down, and bury the body; and, after he was dead, they did it.

"Cap'n Eb he was one of a party o' eight that pulled down the chimbley; and there, sure enough, was the skeleton of poor Lommedieu.

"So, there you see, boys, there can't be no iniquity so hid but what it'll come out. The wild Indians of the forest, and the stormy winds and tempests, j'ined together to bring out this 'ere."

"For my part," said Aunt Lois sharply, "I never believed that story."

"Why, Lois," said my grandmother, "Cap'n Eb Sawin was a regular church-member, and a most respectable man."

"Law, mother! I don't doubt he thought so. I suppose he and Cack got drinking toddy together, till he got asleep, and dreamed it. I wouldn't believe such a thing if it did happen right before my face and eyes. I should only think I was crazy, that's all."

"Come, Lois, if I was you, I wouldn't talk so like a Sadducee," said my grandmother. "What would become of all the accounts in Dr. Cotton Mather's *Magnilly* if folks were like you?"

"Wal," said Sam Lawson, drooping contemplatively over the coals, and gazing into the fire. "there's a putty consid'able sight o' things in this world that's true; and then ag'in there's a sight o' things that ain't true. Now, my old gran'ther used to say, 'Boys,' says he, 'if ye want to lead a pleasant and prosperous life, ye must contrive allers to keep jest the happy medium between truth and falsehood.' Now, that are's my doctrine."

Aunt Lois knit severely.

"Boys," said Sam, "don't you want ter go down with me and get a mug o' cider?"

Of course, we did, and took down a basket to bring up some apples to roast.

"Boys," says Sam mysteriously, while he was drawing the cider, "you jest ask your Aunt Lois to tell you what she knows 'bout Ruth Sullivan."

"Why, what is it?"

"Oh! you must ask *her*. These 'ere folks that's so kind o' toppin' about sperits and sich, come sift 'em down, you gen'lly find they knows one story that kind o' puzzles 'em. Now you mind, and jist ask your Aunt Lois about Ruth Sullivan."

The Sullivan Looking-Glass

"Aunt Lois," said I, "what was that story about Ruth Sullivan?"

Aunt Lois's quick black eyes gave a surprised flash; and she and my grandmother looked at each other a minute significantly.

"Who told you anything about Ruth Sullivan," she said sharply.

"Nobody. Somebody said *you* knew something about her," said I.

I was holding a skein of yarn for Aunt Lois; and she went on winding in silence, putting the ball through loops and tangled places.

"Little boys shouldn't ask questions," she concluded at last sententiously. "Little boys that ask too many questions get sent to bed."

I knew that of old, and rather wondered at my own hardihood.

Aunt Lois wound on in silence; but, looking in her face, I could see plainly that I had started an exciting topic.

"I should think," pursued my grandmother in her corner, "that Ruth's case might show you, Lois, that a good many things may happen—more than you believe."

"Oh, well, mother! Ruth's was a strange case; but I suppose there are ways of accounting for it."

"You believed Ruth, didn't you?"

"Oh, certainly, I believed Ruth! Why shouldn't I? Ruth was one of my best friends, and as true a girl as lives: there wasn't any nonsense about Ruth. She was one of the sort," said Aunt Lois reflectively, "that I'd as soon trust as myself: when she said a thing was so and so, I knew it was so."

"Then, if you think Ruth's story was true," pursued my grandmother, "what's the reason you are always cavilling at things just 'cause you can't understand how they came to be so?"

Aunt Lois set her lips firmly, and wound with grim resolve. She was the very impersonation of that obstinate rationalism that grew up at the New-England fireside, close alongside of the most undoubting faith in the supernatural.

"I don't believe such things," at last she snapped out, "and I don't disbelieve them. I just let 'em alone. What do I know about 'em? Ruth tells me a story; and I believe her. I know what she saw beforehand, came true in a most remarkable way. Well, I'm sure I've no objection. One thing may be true, or another, for all me; but just because I believe Ruth Sullivan, I'm not going to believe, right and left, all the stories in Cotton Mather, and all that anybody can hawk up to tell. Not I."

This whole conversation made me all the more curious to get at the story thus dimly indicated; and so, we beset Sam for information.

"So, your Aunt Lois wouldn't tell ye nothin'," said Sam. "Wanter know, neow! sho!"

"No: she said we must go to bed if we asked her."

"That 'are's a way folks has; but, ye see, boys," said Sam, while a droll confidential expression crossed the lack-lustre dolefulness of his visage, "ye see, I put ye up to it, 'cause Miss Lois is so large and commandin' in her ways, and so kind o' up and down in all her doin's, that I like once and a while to sort o' gravel her; and I knowed enough to know that that 'are question would git her in a tight place.

"Ye see, yer Aunt Lois was knowin' to all this 'ere about Ruth, so there wer'n't no gettin' away from it; and it's about as remarkable a providence as any o' them of Mister Cotton Marther's *Magnilly*. So, if you'll come up in the barn-chamber this arternoon, where I've got a lot o' flax to hatchel out, I'll tell ye all about it."

So that afternoon beheld Sam arranged at full length on a pile of top-tow in the barn-chamber, hatchelling by proxy by putting Harry and myself to the service.

Wal, now, boys, it's kind o' refreshing to see how wal ye take hold," he observed. "Nothin' like bein' industrious while ye'r young: gret sight better now than loafin off, down in them medders.

"'*In books and work and useful play*
Let my fust years be past:
So, shall I give for every day
Some good account at last.'"

"But, Sam, if we work for you, you must tell us that story about Ruth Sullivan."

"Lordy massy! yis—course I will. I've had the best kind o' chances of knowin' all about that 'are. Wal, you see there was old Gineral Sullivan, he lived in state and grande'r in the old Sullivan house out to Roxberry. I been to Roxberry, and seen that 'are house o' Gineral Sullivan's. There was one time that I was a consid'able spell lookin' round in Roxberry, a kind o seein' how things wuz there, and whether or no there mightn't be some sort o' providential openin' or suthin'. I used to stay with Aunt Polly Ginger. She was sister to Mehitable Ginger, Gineral Sullivan's housekeeper, and hed the in and out o' the Sullivan house, and kind o' kept the run o' how things went and came in it. Polly she was a kind o' cousin o' my mother's, and allers glad to see me.

"Fact was, I was putty handy round house; and she used to save up her broken things and sich till I come round in the fall; and then I'd mend 'em up, and put the clock right, and split her up a lot o' kindlings, and board up the cellar-windows, and kind o' make her sort o' comfortable,—she bein' a lone body and no man round. As I said, it was sort o' convenient to hev me; and so I jest got the run o' things in the Sullivan house pretty much as ef I was one on 'em. Gineral Sullivan he kept a grand house, I tell you. You see, he cum from the old country, and felt sort o' lordly and grand; and they used to hev the gretest kind o' doin's there to the Sullivan house. Ye ought ter a seen that 'are house,—gret big front hall and gret wide stairs; none o' your steep kind that breaks a feller's neck to get up and down, but gret broad stairs with easy risers, so they used to say you could a cantered a pony up that 'are stairway easy as not.

"Then there was gret wide rooms, and sofys, and curtains, and gret curtained bedsteads that looked sort o' like fortifications, and pictur's that was got in Italy and Rome and all them 'are heathen places. Ye see, the Gineral was a drefful worldly old critter, and was all for the pomps and the vanities. Lordy massy! I wonder what the poor old critter thinks about it all now, when his body's all gone to dust and ashes in the graveyard, and his soul's gone to 'tarnity! Wal, that 'are ain't none o' my business; only it shows the vanity o' riches in a kind o' strikin' light, and makes me content that I never hed none."

"But, Sam, I hope General Sullivan wasn't a wicked man, was he?"

"Wal, I wouldn't say he was railly wickeder than the run; but he was one o' these 'ere high-stepping, big-feeling fellers, that seem to be a hevin' their portion in this life. Drefful proud he was; and he was pretty much sot on this world, and kep' a sort o' court goin' on round him. Wal, I don't jedge him nor nobody: folks that hes the world is apt to get sot on it. Don't none on us do more than middlin' well."

"But, Sam, what about Ruth Sullivan?"

"Ruth?—Oh, yis!—Ruth—

"Wal, ye see, the only crook in the old Gineral's lot was he didn't hev no children. Mis' Sullivan, she was a beautiful woman, as handsome as a pictur'; but she never had but one child; and he was a son who died when he was a baby, and about broke her heart. And then this 'ere Ruth was her sister's child, that was born about the same time; and, when the boy died, they took Ruth home to sort o' fill his place, and kind o' comfort up Mis' Sullivan. And then Ruth's father and mother died; and they adopted her for their own, and brought her up.

"Wal, she grew up to be amazin' handsome. Why, everybody said that she was jest the light and glory of that 'are old Sullivan place, and worth more'n all the pictur's and the silver and the jewels, and all there was in the house; and she was jest so innercent and sweet, that you never see nothing to beat it. Wal, your Aunt Lois she got acquainted with Ruth one summer when she was up to Old Town a visitin' at Parson Lothrop's. Your Aunt Lois was a gal then, and a pretty good-lookin' one too; and, somehow or other, she took to Ruth, and Ruth took to her. And when Ruth went home, they used to be a writin' backwards and forads; and I guess the fact was, Ruth thought about as much of your Aunt Lois as she did o' anybody. Ye see, your aunt was a kind o' strong up-and-down woman that always knew certain jest what she did know; and Ruth, she was one o' them gals that seems sort o' like a stray lamb or a dove that's sort o' lost their way in the world, and wants someone to show 'em where to go next.

"For, ye see, the fact was, the old Gineral and Madam, they didn't agree very well. He wa'n't well pleased that she didn't have no children; and she was sort o' jealous o' him 'cause she got hold o' some sort of story about how he was to a married somebody else over there in England: so she got sort o' riled up, jest as wimmen will, the best on 'em; and they was pretty apt to have spats, and one could give t'other as good as they sent; and, by all accounts, they fit putty lively sometimes. And, between the two, Ruth she was sort o' scared, and fluttered like a dove that didn't know jest where to settle. Ye see, there she was in that 'are great wide house, where they was a feastin' and a prancin' and a dancin', and a goin' on like Ahashuerus and Herodias and all them old Scriptur' days. There was a comin' and goin,' and there was gret dinners and gret doin's, but no love; and, you know, the Scriptur' says, 'Better is a dinner o' yarbs, where love is, than a stalled ox, and hatred therewith.'

"Wal, I don't orter say *hatred*, arter all. I kind o' reckon, the old Gineral did the best he could: the fact is, when a woman gits a kink in her head agin a man, the best on us don't alters do jest the right thing.

"Anyway, Ruth, she was sort o' forlorn, and didn't seem to take no comfort in the goin's on. The Gineral he was mighty fond on her, and proud on her; and there wa'n't nothin' too good for Ruth. He was free-handed, the Gineral wuz. He dressed her up in silks and satins, and she hed a maid to wait on her, and she hed sets o' pearl and dimond; and Madam Sullivan she thought all the world on her, and kind o' worshipped the ground she trod on. And yet Ruth was sort o' lonesome.

"Ye see, Ruth wa'n't calculated for grande'r, some folks ain't.

"Why, that 'are summer she spent out to Old Town, she was jest as chirk and chipper as a wren, a wearin' her little sun-bun-net, and goin' a huckle-berryin' and a black-berryin' and diggin' sweet-flag, and gettin cowslops and dandelions; and she hed a word for everybody. And everybody liked Ruth, and wished her well. Wal, she was sent for her health; and she got that, and more too: she got a sweetheart.

"Ye see, there was a Cap'n Oliver a visitin' at the minister's that summer—a nice, handsome young man as ever was. He and Ruth and your Aunt Lois, they was together a good deal; and they was a ramblin' and a ridin' and a sailin': and so Ruth and the capting went the way o' all the airth, and fell dead in love with each other. Your Aunt Lois she was knowing to it and all about it, 'cause Ruth she was jest one of them that couldn't take a step without somebody to talk to.

"Captain Oliver was of a good family in England; and so, when he made bold to ask the old Gineral for Ruth, he didn't say him nay: and it was agreed, as they was young, they should wait a year or two. If he and she was of the same mind, he should be free to marry her. Jest right on that, the captain's regiment was ordered home, and he had to go; and, the next they heard, it was sent off to India. And poor little Ruth she kind o' drooped and pined; but she kept true, and wouldn't have nothin' to say to nobody that came arter her, for there was lots and cords o' fellows as did come arter her. Ye see, Ruth had a takin' way with her; and then she had the name of bein' a great heiress, and that alters draws fellers, as molasses does flies.

"Wal, then the news came, that Captain Oliver was comin' home to England, and the ship was took by the Algerenes, and he was gone into slavery there among them heathen Mahomedans and what not.

"Folks seemed to think it was all over with him, and Ruth might jest as well give up fust as last. And the old Gineral he'd come to think she might do better; and he kep' a introducin' one and another, and tryin' to marry her off; but Ruth she wouldn't. She used to write sheets and sheets to your Aunt Lois about it; and I think Aunt Lois she kep' her grit up. Your Aunt Lois she'd a stuck by a man to the end o' time ef't ben her case; and so, she told Ruth.

"Wal, then there was young Jeff Sullivan, the Gineral's nephew, he turned up; and the Gineral he took a gret fancy to him. He was next heir to the Gineral; but he'd ben a pretty rackety youngster in his young days—off to sea, and what not, and sowed a consid'able crop o' wild oats. People said he'd been a pirating off there in South Ameriky. Lordy massy! nobody rightly knew where he hed ben or where he hadn't: all was, he turned up at last all alive, and chipper as a skunk blackbird. Wal, of course he made his court to Ruth; and the Gineral, he rather backed him up in it; but Ruth she wouldn't have nothin' to say to him. Wal, he come and took up his lodgin' at the Gineral's; and he was jest as slippery as an eel, and sort o' slid into everything, that was a goin' on in the house and about it. He was here, and he was there, and he was everywhere, and a havin' his say about this and that; and he got everybody putty much under his thumb. And they used to say, he wound the Gineral round and round like a skein o' yarn; but he couldn't come it round Ruth.

"Wal, the Gineral said she shouldn't be forced; and Jeff, he was smooth as satin, and said he'd be willing to wait as long as Jacob did for Rachel. And so there he sot down, a watchin' as patient as a cat at a mouse-hole: 'cause the Gineral he was thickset and short-necked, and drank pretty free, and was one o' the sort that might pop off any time.

29

"Wal, Mis' Sullivan, she beset the Gineral to make a provision for Ruth; 'cause she told him very sensible, that he'd brought her up in luxury, and that it wa'n't fair not to settle somethin' on her; and so the Gineral he said he'd make a will, and part the property equally between them. And he says to Jeff, that, if he played his part as a young fellow oughter know how, it would all come to him in the end; 'cause they hadn't heard nothing from Captain Oliver for three or four years, and folks about settled it that he must be dead.

"Wal, the Gineral he got a letter about an estate that had come to him in England; and he had to go over. Wal, livin' on the next estate, was the very cousin of the Gineral's that he was to a married when they was both young: the lands joined so that the grounds run together. What came between them two nobody knows; but she never married, and there she was. There was high words between the Gineral and Madam Sullivan about his goin' over. She said there wa'n't no sort o' need on't, and he said there was; and she said she hoped she should be in her grave afore he come back; and he said she might suit herself about that for all him. That 'are was the story that the housekeeper told to Aunt Polly; and Aunt Polly she told me. These 'ere squabbles somehow allers does kind o' leak out one way or t'other.

"Anyhow, it was a house divided agin itself at the Gineral's, when he was a fixin' out for the voyage. There was Ruth a goin' fust to one, and then to t'other, and tryin' all she could to keep peace between 'em; and there was this 'ere Master Slick Tongue talkin' this way to one side, and that way to t'other, and the old Gineral kind c' like a shuttle-cock atween 'em.

"Wal, then, the night afore he sailed, the Gineral he hed his lawyer up in his library there, a lookin' over all his papers and bonds and things, and a witnessing his will; and Master Jeff was there, as lively as a cricket, a goin' into all affairs, and offerin' to take precious good care while he was gone; and the Gineral he had his papers and letters out, a sortin' on 'em over, which was to be took to the old country, and which was to be put in a trunk to go back to Lawyer Dennis's office.

"Wal, Abner Ginger, Polly's boy, he that was footman and waiter then at the Gineral's, he told me, that, about eight o'clock that evening he went up with hot water and lemons and sperits and sich, and he see the gret green table in the library all strewed and covered with piles o' papers; and there was tin boxes a standin' round; and the Gineral a packin' a trunk, and young Master-Jeff, as lively and helpful as a rat that smells cheese. And then the Gineral he says, 'Abner,' says he, 'can you write your name?'—'I should hope so, Gineral.' says Abner.—'Wal, then Abner,' says he, 'this is my last will; and I want you to witness it,' and so Abner he put down his name opposite to a place with a wafer and a seal; and then the Gineral, he says, 'Abner, you tell Ginger to come here.' That, you see, was his housekeeper, my Aunt Polly's sister, and a likely woman as ever was.

"And so, they had her up, and she put down her name to the will; and then Aunt Polly she was had up (she was drinking tea there that night), and she put down her name. And all of 'em did it with good heart, 'cause it had got about among 'em that the will was to provide for Miss Ruth; for everybody loved Ruth, ye see, and there was consid'ble many stories kind o' goin' the rounds about Master Jeff and his doin's. And they did say he sort o' kep' up the strife atween the Gineral and my lady, and so they didn't think none too well o' him; and, as he was next o' kin, and Miss Ruth wa'n't none o' the Gineral's blood (ye see, she was Mis' Sullivan's sister's child), of course there wouldn't nothin' go to Miss Ruth in way o' law, and so that was why the signin' o' that 'are will was so much talked about among 'em."

"Wal, you see, the Gineral he sailed the next day; and Jeff he staid by to keep watch o' things.

"Wal, the old Gineral he got over safe; for Miss Sullivan, she had a letter from him all right. When he got away, his conscience sort o' nagged him, and he was minded to be a good husband. At any rate, he wrote a good loving letter to her, and sent his love to Ruth, and sent over lots o' little keepsakes and things for her, and told her that he left her under good protection, and wanted her to try and make up her mind to marry Jeff, as that would keep the property together.

"Wal, now there couldn't be no sort o' sugar sweeter than Jeff was to them lone wimmen. Jeff was one o' the sort that could be all things to all wimmen. He waited and he tended, and he was as humble as any snake in the grass that ever ye see and the old lady, she clean fell in with him, but Ruth, she seemed to have a regular spite agin him. And she that war as gentle as a lamb, that never had so much as a hard thought of a mortal critter, and wouldn't tread on a worm, she was so set agin Jeff, that she wouldn't so much as touch his hand when she got out o' her kerridge.

"Wal, now comes the strange part o' my story. Ruth was one o' the kind that *hes the gift o' seein'. She was born with a veil over her face!*"

This mysterious piece of physiological information about Ruth was given with a look and air that announced something very profound and awful; and we both took up the inquiry, "Born with a veil over her face? How should *that* make her see?"

"Wal, boys, how should I know? But the fact is so. There's those as is wal known as hes the gift o' seem' what others can't see: they can see through walls and houses; they can see people's hearts; they can see what's to come. They don't know nothin' how 'tis, but this 'ere knowledge comes to 'em: it's a gret gift; and that sort's born with the veil over their faces. Ruth was o' these 'ere. Old Granny Badger she was the knowingest old nuss in all these parts; and she was with Ruth's mother when she was born, and she told Lady Lothrop all about it. Says she, 'You may depend upon it that child'll have the "*second-sight*,"' says she. Oh, that 'are fact was wal known! Wal, that was the reason why Jeff Sullivan couldn't come it round Ruth tho' he was silkier than a milkweed-pod, and jest about as patient as a spider in his hole a watchin' to get his grip on a fly. Ruth wouldn't argue with him, and she wouldn't flout him; but she jest shut herself up in herself, and kept a lookout on him; but she told your Aunt Lois jest what she thought about him.

"Wal, in about six months, come the news that the Gineral

was dead. He dropped right down in his tracks, dead with apoplexy, as if he had been shot; and Lady Maxwell she writ a long letter to my lady and Ruth. Ye see, he'd got to be Sir Thomas Sullivan over there; and he was a comin' home to take 'em all over to England to live in grande'r. Wal, my Lady Sullivan (she was then, ye see) she took it dreffal hard. Ef they'd a been the lovingest couple in the world, she coulau't a took it harder. Aunt Polly, she said it was all 'cause she thought so much of him, that she fit him so. There's women that thinks so much o' their husbands, that they won't let 'em hev no peace o' their life; and I expect it war so with her poor soul! Anyway, she went right down smack when she heard he was dead. She was abed, sick, when the news come; and she never spoke nor smiled, jest turned her back to everybody, and kinder wilted and wilted, and was dead in a week. And there was poor little Ruth left all alone in the world, with neither kith nor kin but Jeff.

"Wal, when the funeral was over, and the time app'inted to read the will and settle up matters, there wa'n't no will to be found nowhere, high nor low.

"Lawyer Dean he flew round like a parched pea on a shovel. He said he thought he could a gone in the darkest night, and put his hand on that 'ere will; but when he went where he thought it was, he found it warn't there, and he knowed he'd kep' it under lock and key. What he thought was the will turned out to be an old mortgage. Wal, there was an awful row and a to-do about it, you may be sure. Ruth, she jist said nothin' good or bad. And her not speakin' made Jeff a sight more uncomfortable than ef she'd a hed it out with him. He told, her it shouldn't make no sort o' difference; that he should allers stand ready to give her all he hed, if she'd only take him with it. And when it came to that she only gin him a look, and went out o' the room.

"Jeff, he flared and flounced and talked, and went round and round a rumpussin' among the papers, but no will was forthcomin', high or low. Wal, now here comes what's remarkable. Ruth, she told this 'ere, all the particulars, to yer Aunt Lois and Lady Lothrop. She said that the night after the funeral she went

up to her chamber. Ruth had the gret front chamber, opposite to Mis' Sullivan's. I've been in it; it was a monstrous big
room, with outlandish furniture in it, that the Gineral brought
over from an old palace out to Italy. And there was a great big
lookin'-glass over the dressin'-table, that they said come from
Venice, that swung so that you could see the whole room in it.
Wal, she was a standin' front o' this, jist goin' to undress herself, a
hearin' the rain drip on the leaves and the wind a whishin' and
whisperin' in the old elm-trees, and jist a thinkin' over her lot,
and what should she do now, all alone in the world, when of a
sudden she felt a kind o' lightness in her head, and she thought
she seemed to see somebody in the glass a movin'.

"And she looked behind, and there wa'n't nobody there.
Then she looked forward in the glass, and saw a strange big
room, that she'd never seen before, with a long, painted winder
in it; and alongside o' this stood a tall cabinet with a good many
drawers in it. And she saw herself, and knew that it was herself,
in this room, along with another woman whose back was turned
towards her. She saw herself speak to this woman, and p'int to
the cabinet. She saw the woman nod her head. She saw herself
go to the cabinet, and open the middle drawer, and take out a
bundle o' papers from the very back end on't. She saw her take
out a paper from the middle, and open it, and hold it up; and she
knew that there was the missin' will. Wal, it all overcome her so
that she fainted clean away. And her maid found her a lyin' front
o' the dressin'-table on the floor.

"She was sick of a fever for a week or fortnight a'ter; and
your Aunt Lois she was down takin' care of her; and, as soon as
she got able to be moved, she was took out to Lady Lothrop's.
Jeff he was jist as attentive and good as he could be; but she
wouldn't bear him near her room. If he so much as set a foot
on the stairs that led to it, she'd know it, and got so wild that he
hed to be kept from comin' into the front o' the house. But he
was doin' his best to buy up good words from everybody. He
paid all the servants double; he kept everyone in their places, and
did so well by 'em all that the gen'l word among 'em was that

Miss Ruth couldn't do better than to marry such a nice, open-handed gentleman.

"Wal, Lady Lothrop she wrote to Lady Maxwell all that hed happened; and Lady Maxwell, she sent over for Ruth to come over and be a companion for her, and said she'd adopt her, and be as a mother to her.

"Wal, then Ruth she went over with some gentlefolks that was goin' back to England, and offered to see her safe and sound; and so, she was set down at Lady Maxwell's manor. It was a grand place, she said, and such as she never see before—like them old gentry places in England. And Lady Maxwell she made much of her, and cosseted her up for the sake of what the old Gineral had said about her. And Ruth she told her all her story, and how she believed that the will was to be found somewhere, and that she should be led to see it yet.

"She told her, too, that she felt it in her that Cap'n Oliver wasn't dead, and that he'd come back yet. And Lady Maxwell she took up for her with might and main, and said she'd stand by her. But then, ye see, so long as there warn't no will to be found, there warn't nothin' to be done. Jeff was the next heir; and he'd got everything, stock, and lot, and the estate in England into the bargain. And folks was beginnin' to think putty well of him, as folks allers does when a body is up in the world, and hes houses and lands. Lordy massy! riches allers covers a multitude o' sins.

"Finally, when Ruth hed ben six months with her, one day Lady Maxwell got to tellin' her all about her history, and what hed ben atween her and her cousin, when they was young, and how they hed a quarrel and he flung off to Ameriky, and all them things that it don't do folks no good to remember when it's all over and can't be helped. But she was a lone body, and it seemed to do her good to talk about it.

"Finally, she says to Ruth, says she, 'I'll show you a room in this house you han't seen before. It was the room where we hed that quarrel,' says she; 'and the last I saw of him was there, till he come back to die,' says she.

"So, she took a gret key out of her bunch; and she led Ruth

along a long passage-way to the other end of the house, and opened on a great library. And the minute Ruth came in, she threw up her hands and gin a great cry. 'Oh!' says she, 'this is the room! and there is the window! and there is the cabinet! *and there in that middle drawer at the back end in a bundle of papers is the will!'*

"And Lady Maxwell she said, quite dazed, 'Go look,' says she. And Ruth went, jest as she seed heself do, and opened the drawer, and drew forth from the back part a yellow pile of old letters. And in the middle of those was the will, sure enough. Ruth drew it out, and opened it, and showed it to her.

"Wal, you see that will give Ruth the whole of the Gineral's property in America, tho' it did leave the English estate to Jeff.

"Wal, the end on't was like a story-book.

"Jeff, he made believe be mighty glad. And he said it must a ben that the Gineral hed got flustered with the sperit and water, and put that 'ere will in among his letters that he was a doin' up to take back to England. For it was in among Lady Maxwell's letters that she writ him when they was young, and that he'd a kep' all these years and was a takin' back to her.

"Wal, Lawyer Dean said he was sure that Jeff made himself quite busy and useful that night, a tyin' up the papers with red tape, and a packin' the Gineral's trunk; and that, when Jeff gin him his bundle to lock up in his box, he never mistrusted but what he'd got it all right.

"Wal, you see it was jest one of them things that can't be known to the jedgment-day. It might a ben an accident, and then agin it might not; and folks settled it one way or t'other, 'cordin' to their 'pinion o' Jeff; but ye see how 'mazin' handy for him it happened! Why, ef it hadn't ben for the providence I've ben a tellin' about, there it might a lain in them old letters, that Lady Maxwell said she never hed the heart to look over! it never would a turned up in the world."

"Well," said I, "what became of Ruth?"

"Oh! Cap'n Oliver he came back all alive, and escaped from the Algerines; and they was married in King's Chapel, and lived in the old Sullivan House, in peace and prosperity. That's jest how the story was; and now Aunt Lois can make what she's a mind ter out on't."

"And what became of Jeff?"

"Oh! he started to go over to England, and the ship was wrecked off the Irish coast, and that was the last of him. He never got to his property."

"Good enough for him," said both of us.

"Wal, I don't know: 'twas pretty hard on Jeff. Mebbe he did, and mebbe he didn't. I'm glad I warn't in his shoes, tho'. I'd rather never hed nothin'. This 'ere hastin' to be rich is sich a dreffru temptation.

"Wal, now, boys, ye've done a nice lot o' flax, and I guess we'll go up to yer grand'ther's cellar and git a mug o' cyder. Talkin' always gits me dry."

Captain Kidd's Money

One of our most favourite legendary resorts was the old barn.
Sam Lawson preferred it on many accounts. It was quiet and
retired, that is to say, at such distance from his own house, that
he could not hear if Hepsy called ever so loudly, and farther off
than it would be convenient for that industrious and painstaking
woman to follow him. Then there was the soft fragrant cushion
of hay, on which his length of limb could be easily bestowed.

Our barn had an upper loft with a swinging outer door that
commanded a view of the old mill, the waterfall, and the distant
windings of the river, with its grassy green banks, its graceful
elm draperies, and its white flocks of water-lilies; and then on
this Saturday afternoon we had Sam all to ourselves. It was a
drowsy, dreamy October day, when the hens were lazily "*craw,
crawing,*" in a soft, conversational undertone with each other, as
they scratched and picked the hay-seed under the barn windows. Below in the barn black Cæsar sat quietly hatchelling flax,
sometimes gurgling and giggling to himself with an overflow of
that interior jollity with which he seemed to be always full. The
African in New England was a curious contrast to everybody
around him in the joy and satisfaction that he seemed to feel
in the mere fact of being alive. Every white person was glad or
sorry for some appreciable cause in the past, present, or future,
which was capable of being definitely stated; but black Cæsar
was in an eternal giggle and frizzle and simmer of enjoyment
for which he could give no earthly reason: he was an "embodied
joy," like Shelley's skylark.

"Jest hear him," said Sam Lawson, looking pensively over the hay-mow, and strewing hayseed down on his wool. "How that 'are critter seems to tickle and laugh all the while 'bout nothin'. Lordy massy! he don't seem never to consider that 'this life's a dream, an empty show.'"

"Look here, Sam," we broke in, anxious to cut short a threatened stream of morality, "you promised to tell us about Capt. Kidd, and how you dug for his money."

"Did I, now? Wal, boys, that 'are history o' Kidd's is a warnin' to fellers. Why, Kidd had pious parents and Bible and sanctuary privileges when he was a boy, and yet come to be hanged. It's all in this 'ere song I'm a goin' to sing ye. Lordy massy! I wish I had my bass-viol now.—Cæsar," he said, calling down from his perch, "can't you strike the pitch o' 'Cap'n Kidd,' on your fiddle?"

Cæsar's fiddle was never far from him. It was, in fact, tucked away in a nice little nook just over the manger; and he often caught an interval from his work to scrape a dancing-tune on it, keeping time with his heels, to our great delight.

A most wailing minor-keyed tune was doled forth, which seemed quite refreshing to Sam's pathetic vein, as he sang in his most lugubrious tones,—

My name was Robert Kidd
As I sailed, as I sailed,
My name was Robert Kidd;
God's laws I did forbid,
And so wickedly I did,
As I sailed, as I sailed.

"Now ye see, boys, he's a goin' to tell how he abused his religious privileges; just hear now:—

My father taught me well,
As I sailed, as I sailed;
My father taught me well
To shun the gates of hell,
But yet I did rebel,

As I sailed, as I sailed.

He put a Bible in my hand,
As I sailed, as I sailed;
He put a Bible in my hand,
And I sunk it in the sand
Before I left the strand,
As I sailed, as I sailed.

"Did ye ever hear o' such a hardened, contrary critter, boys? It's awful to think on. Wal, ye see that 'are's the way fellers allers begin the ways o' sin, by turnin' their backs on the Bible and the advice o' pious parents. Now hear what he come to:—

Then I murdered William More,
As I sailed, as I sailed;
I murdered William More,
And left him in his gore,
Not many leagues from shore,
As I sailed, as I sailed.

To execution dock
I must go, I must go.
To execution dock,
While thousands round me flock,
To see me on the block,
I must go, I must go.

"There was a good deal more on't," said Sam, pausing, "but I don't seem to remember it; but it's real solemn and affectin'."

"Who was Capt. Kidd, Sam?" said I.

"Wal, he was an officer in the British navy, and he got to bein' a pirate: used to take ships and sink 'em, and murder the folks; and so they say he got no end o' money,—gold and silver and precious stones, as many as the wise men in the East. But ye see, what good did it all do him? He couldn't use it, and dar'sn't keep it; so, he used to bury it in spots round here and there in the awfullest heathen way ye ever heard of. Why, they say he allers used to kill one or two men or women or children of his prisoners, and bury with it, so that their sperits might keep watch on it ef anybody was to dig arter it. That 'are thing has been tried and tried and tried, but no man nor mother's son on 'em ever got a cent that dug. 'Twas tried here'n Oldtown; and they come pretty nigh gettin' on't, but it gin 'em the slip. Ye see, boys, *it's the Devil's money*, and he holds a pretty tight grip on't."

"Well, how was it about digging for it? Tell us, did you do it? Were you there? Did you see it? And why couldn't they get it?" we both asked eagerly and in one breath.

"Why, Lordy massy! boys, your questions tumbles over each other thick as martins out o' a martin-box. Now, you jest be moderate and let alone, and I'll tell you all about it from the beginnin' to the end. I didn't railly have no hand in't, though I was know-in' to 't, as I be to most things that goes on round here; but my conscience wouldn't railly a let me start on no sich undertakin'.

"Wal, the one that fust sot the thing a goin' was old Mother Hokum, that used to live up in that little tumble-down shed by the cranberry-pond up beyond the spring pastur'. They had a putty bad name, them Hokums. How they got a livin' nobody knew; for they didn't seem to pay no attention to raisin' nothin' but childun, but the duce knows, there was plenty o' them. Their old hut was like a rabbit-pen: there was a tow-head to every crack and cranny. 'Member what old Cæsar said once when the word come to the store that old Hokum had got twins. 'S'pose de Lord knows best,' says Cæsar, 'but *I* thought dere was Ho-kums enough afore.'

"Wal, even poor workin' industrious folks like me finds it's hard gettin' along when there's so many mouths to feed. Lordy massy! there don't never seem to be no end on't, and so it ain't wonderful, come to think on't, ef folks like them Hokums gets tempted to help along in ways that ain't quite right. Anyhow, folks did use to think that old Hokum was too sort o' familiar with their wood-piles 'long in the night, though they couldn't never prove it on him; and when Mother Hokum come to houses round to wash, folks use sometimes to miss pieces, here and there, though they never could find 'em on her; then they was allers a gettin' in debt here and a gottin' in debt there. Why, they got to owin' two dollars to Joe Gidger for butcher's meat. Joe was sort o' good-natured and let 'em have meat, 'cause Hokum he promised so fair to pay; but he couldn't never get it out o' him. 'Member once Joe walked clear up to the cranberry-pond artor that 'are two dollars; but Mother Hokum she see him a comin' jest as he come past the juniper-bush on the corner. She says to Hokum, 'Get into bed, old man, quick, and let me tell the story,' says she.

"So she covered him up; and when Gidger come in she come up to him, and says she, 'Why, Mr. Gidger, I'm jest ashamed to see ye: why, Mr. Hokum was jest a comin' down to pay ye that 'are money last week, but ye see he was took down with the smallpox'—Joe didn't hear no more: he just turned round, and he streaked it out that 'are door with his coat-tails flyin' out straight ahind him; and old Mother Hokum she jest stood at the window holdin' her sides and laughin' fit to split, to see him run. That 'are's jest a sample o' the ways them Hokums cut up.

"Wal, you see, boys, there's a queer kind o' rock down on the bank o' the river, that looks sort o' like a grave-stone. The biggest part on't is sunk down under ground, and it's pretty well growed over with blackberry-vines; but, when you scratch the bushes away, they used to make out some queer marks on that 'are rock. They was sort o' lines and crosses; and folks would have it that them was Kidd's private marks, and that there was one o' the places where he hid his money.

"Wal, there's no sayin' fairly how it come to be thought so; but fellers used to say so, and they used sometimes to talk it over to the tahvern, and kind o' wonder whether or no, if they should dig, they wouldn't come to suthin'.

"Wal, old Mother Hokum she heard on't, and she was a sort o' enterprisin' old crittur: fact was, she had to be, 'cause the young Hokums was jest like bag-worms, the more they growed the more they eat, and I expect she found it pretty hard to fill their mouths; and so she said ef there was anything under that 'are rock, they'd as good's have it as the Devil; and so she didn't give old Hokum no peace o' his life, but he must see what there was there.

"Wal, I was with 'em the night they was a talkin' on't up. Ye see, Hokum he got thirty-seven cents' worth o' lemons and sperit. I see him goin' by as I was out a splittin' kindlin's; and says he, 'Sam, you jest go 'long up to our house tonight,' says he: 'Toddy Whitney and Harry Wiggin's comin' up, and we're goin' to have a little suthin' hot,' says he; and he kind o' showed me the lemons and sperit. And I told him I guessed I would go 'long. Wal, I kind o' wanted to see what they'd be up to, ye know.

"Wal, come to find out, they was a talkin' about Cap'n Kidd's treasures, and layin' out how they should get it, and a settin' one another on with gret stories about it.

"'I've heard that there was whole chists full o' gold guineas,' says one.

"'And I've heard o' gold bracelets and ear-rings and finger-rings all sparklin' with diamonds,' says another.

"'Maybe it's old silver plate from some o' them old West Indian *grandees*,' says another.

"'Wal, whatever it is,' says Mother Hokum, 'I want to be into it,' says she.

"'Wal, Sam, won't you jine?' says they.

"'Wal, boys,' says I, 'I kind o' don't feel jest like j'inin'. I sort o' ain't clear about the rights on't: seems to me it's mighty nigh like goin' to the Devil for money.'

"'Wal,' says Mother Hokum, 'what if 'tis? Money's money, get it how ye will; and the Devil's money'll buy as much meat as any. I'd go to the Devil, if he gave good money.'

"'Wal, I guess I wouldn't,' says I. 'Don't you 'member the sermon Parson Lothrop preached about hastin' to be rich, last sabba' day?'

"'Parson Lothrop be hanged!' says she. 'Wal, now,' says she, 'I like to see a parson with his silk stockin's and great gold-headed cane, a lollopin' on his carriage behind his fat, prancin' hosses, comin' to meetin' to preach to us poor folks not to want to be rich! How'd he like it to have forty-'leven children, and nothin' to put onto 'em or into 'em, I wonder? Guess if Lady Lothrop had to rub and scrub, and wear her fingers to the bone as I do, she'd want to be rich; and I guess the parson, if he couldn't get a bellyful for a week, would be for diggin' up Kidd's money, or doing 'most anything else to make the pot bile.'

"'Wal,' says I, 'I'll kind o' go with ye, boys, and sort o' see how things turn out; but I guess I won't take no shere in't,' says I.

"Wal, they got it all planned out. They was to wait till the full moon, and then they was to get Primus King to go with 'em and help do the diggin'. Ye see, Hokum and Toddy Whitney and Wiggin are all putty softly fellers, and hate dreffully to work; and I tell you the Kidd money ain't to be got without a pretty tough piece o' diggin. Why, it's jest like diggin' a well to get at it. Now, Primus King was the master hand for diggin' wells, and so they said they'd get him by givin' on him a shere.

"Harry Wiggin, he didn't want no n———r a sherin' in it, he said; but Toddy and Hokum they said that when there was such stiff diggin' to be done, they didn't care if they did go in with a n———.

"Wal, Wiggin he said he hadn't no objection to havin' the n———r do the diggin,' it was *sherin' the profits* he objected to.

"'Wal,' says Hokum, 'you can't get him without,' says he. 'Primus knows too much,' says he: 'you can't fool him.' Finally, they 'greed that they was to give Primus twenty dollars, and shere the treasure 'mong themselves.

"Come to talk with Primus, he wouldn't stick in a spade, unless they'd pay him aforehand. Ye see, Primus was up to 'em; he knowed about Gidger, and there wa'n't none on 'em that was particular good pay; and so they all jest hed to rake and scrape, and pay him down the twenty dollars among 'em; and they 'greed for the fust full moon, at twelve' o'clock at night, the 9th of October.

"Wal, ye see I had to tell Hepsy I was goin' out to watch. Wal, so I was; but not jest in the way she took it: but, Lordy massy! a feller has to tell his wife suthin' to keep her quiet, ye know, 'specially Hepsy.

"Wal, wal, of all the moonlight nights that ever I did see, I never did see one equal to that. Why, you could see the colour o' everything. I 'member I could see how the huckleberry-bushes on the rock was red as blood when the moonlight shone through 'em; 'cause the leaves, you see, had begun to turn.

"Goin' on our way we got to talkin' about the sperits.

"'I ain't afraid on 'em,' says Hokum. 'What harm can a sperit do me?' says he. 'I don't care ef there's a dozen on 'em;' and he took a swig at his bottle.

"'Oh! there ain't no sperits,' says Harry Wiggin. 'That 'are talk's all nonsense;' and he took a swig at *his* bottle.

"'Wal,' says Toddy, 'I don't know 'bout that 'are. Me and Ike Sanders has seen the sperits in the Cap'n Brown house. We thought we'd jest have a peek into the window one night; and there was a whole flock o' black colts without no heads on come rushin' on us and knocked us flat.'

"'I expect you'd been at the tahvern,' said Hokum.

"'Wal, yes, we had; but them was sperits: we wa'n't drunk, now; we was jest as sober as ever we was.'

"'Wal, they won't get away my money,' says Primus, 'for I put it safe away in Dinah's teapot afore I come out;' and then he showed all his ivories from ear to ear. 'I think all this 'are's sort o' foolishness,' says Primus.

"'Wal,' says I, 'boys, I ain't a goin' to have no part or lot in this 'ere matter, but I'll jest lay it off to you how it's to be done. Ef Kidd's money is under this rock, there's *sperits* that watch it, and you mustn't give 'em no advantage. There mustn't be a word spoke from the time ye get sight o' the treasure till ye get it safe up on to firm ground,' says I. 'Ef ye do, it'll vanish right out o' sight. I've talked with them that has dug down to it and seen it; but they allers lost it, 'cause they'd call out and say suthin'; and the minute they spoke, away it went.'

"Wal, so they marked off the ground; and Primus he begun to dig, and the rest kind o' sot round. It was so still it was kind o' solemn. Ye see, it was past twelve o'clock, and every critter in

Oldtown was asleep; and there was two whippoorwills on the great Cap'n Brown elm-trees, that kep' a answerin' each other back and forward sort o' solitary like; and then every once in a while there'd come a sort o' strange whisper up among the elm-tree leaves, jest as if there was talkin' goin' on; and every time Primus struck his spade into the ground it sounded sort o' holler, jest as if he'd been a diggin' a grave.

"'It's kind o' melancholy,' says I, 'to think o' them poor critters that had to be killed and buried jest to keep this 'ere treasure. What awful things'll be brought to light in the judgment day! Them poor critters they loved to live and hated to die as much as any on us; but no, they hed to die jest to satisfy that critter's wicked will. I've heard them as thought they could tell the Cap'n Kidd places by layin' their ear to the ground at midnight, and they'd hear groans and wailin's.'"

"Why, Sam! were there really people who could tell where Kidd's money was?" I here interposed.

"Oh, sartin! why, yis. There was Shebna Basconx, he was one. Shebna could always tell what was under the earth. He'd cut a hazel-stick, and hold it in his hand when folks was wantin' to know where to dig wells; and that 'are stick would jest turn in his hand, and p'int down till it would fairly grind the bark off; and ef you dug in that place you was sure to find a spring. Oh, yis! Shebna he's told many where the Kidd money was, and been with 'em when they dug for it; but the pester on't was they allers lost it, 'cause they would some on 'em speak afore they thought."

"But, Sam, what about this digging? Let's know what came of it," said we, as Sam appeared to lose his way in his story.

"Wal, ye see, they dug down about five feet, when Primus he struck his spade smack on something that chincked like iron.

"Wal, then Hokum and Toddy Whitney was into the hole in a minute: they made Primus get out, and they took the spade, 'cause they wanted to be sure to come on it themselves.

"Wal, they begun, and they dug and he scraped, and sure enough they come to a gret iron pot as big as your granny's

" They dug down about five feet."

dinner-pot, with an iron bale to it.

"Wal, then they put down a rope, and he put the rope through the handle; then Hokum and Toddy they clambered upon the bank, and all on 'em began to draw, up jest as still and silent as could be. They drawed and they drawed, till they jest got it even with the ground, when Toddy spoke out all in a tremble, 'There,' says he, '*we've got it!*' And the minit he spoke they was both struck by *suthin* that knocked 'em clean over; and the rope give a crack like a pistol-shot, and broke short off; and the pot went down, down, down, and they heard it goin', *jink, jink, jink;* and it went way down into the earth, and the ground closed over it; and then they heard the screechin'est laugh ye ever did hear."

"I want to know, Sam, did you see that pot?" I exclaimed at this part of the story.

"Wal, no, I didn't. Ye see, I jest happened to drop asleep while they was diggin', I was so kind o' tired, and I didn't wake up till it was all over.

"I was waked up, 'cause there was consid'able of a scuffle; for Hokum was so mad at Toddy for speakin', that he was a fistin' on him; and old Primus he jest haw-hawed and laughed. 'Wal, I got *my* money safe, anyhow,' says he.

"'Wal, come to,' says I. ''Tain't no use cryin' for spilt milk: you've jest got to turn in now and fill up this 'ere hole, else the selectmen'll be down on ye.'

"'Wal,' says Primus, 'I didn't engage to fill up no holes;' and he put his spade on his shoulder and trudged off.

"Wal, it was putty hard work, fillin' in that hole; but Hokum and Toddy and Wiggin had to do it, 'cause they didn't want to have everybody a laughin' at 'em; and I kind o' tried to set it home to 'em, showin' on 'em that 'twas all for the best.

"'Ef you'd a been left to get that 'are money, there'd a come a cuss with it,' says I. 'It shows the vanity o' hastin' to be rich.'

"'Oh, you shet up!' says Hokum, says he. 'You never hasted to anything,' says he. Ye see, he was riled, that's why he spoke so."

"Sam," said we, after maturely reflecting over the story, "what do you suppose was in that pot?"

"Lordy massy! boys: ye never will be done askin' questions. Why, how should I know?"

The Ghost in the Cap'n Brown House

"Now, Sam, tell us certain true, is there any such things as ghosts?"

"Be there ghosts?" said Sam, immediately translating into his vernacular grammar: "wal, now, that 'are's jest the question, ye see."

"Well, grandma thinks there are, and Aunt Lois thinks it's all nonsense. Why, Aunt Lois don't even believe the stories in Cotton Mather's *Magnalia*."

"Wanter know?" said Sam, with a tone of slow, languid meditation.

We were sitting on a bank of the Charles River, fishing. The soft melancholy red of evening was fading off in streaks on the glassy water, and the houses of Oldtown were beginning to loom through the gloom, solemn and ghostly. There are times and tones and moods of nature that make all the vulgar, daily real seem shadowy, vague, and supernatural, as if the outlines of this hard material present were fading into the invisible and unknown. So Oldtown, with its elm-trees, its great square white houses, its meeting-house and tavern and blacksmith's shop and mill, which at high noon seem as real and as commonplace as possible, at this hour of the evening were dreamy and solemn. They rose up blurred, indistinct, dark; here and there winking candles sent long lines of light through the shadows, and little drops of unforeseen rain rippled the sheeny darkness of the water.

"Wal, you see, boys, in them things it's jest as well to mind your granny. There's a consid'able sight o' gumption in grandmas. You look at the folks that's allus tellin' you what they don't believe—they don't believe this, and they don't believe that—and what sort o' folks is they? Why, like yer Aunt Lois, sort o' stringy and dry. There ain't no 'sorption got out o' not believin' nothin'.

"Lord a massy! we don't know nothin' 'bout them things. We hain't ben there, and can't say that there ain't no ghosts and sich; can we, now?"

We agreed to that fact, and sat a little closer to Sam in the gathering gloom.

"Tell us about the Cap'n Brown house, Sam."

"Ye didn't never go over the Cap'n Brown house?"

No, we had not that advantage.

"Wal, yer see, Cap'n Brown he made all his money to sea, in furrin parts, and then come here to Oldtown to settle down.

"Now, there ain't no knowin' 'bout these 'ere old ship-masters, where they's ben, or what they's ben a doin', or how they got their money. Ask me no questions, and I'll tell ye no lies, is 'bout the best philosophy for them. Wal, it didn't do no good to ask Cap'n Brown questions too close, 'cause you didn't git no satisfaction. Nobody rightly knew 'bout who his folks was, or where they come from; and, ef a body asked him, he used to say that the very fust he know'd 'bout himself he was a young man walkin' the streets in London.

"But, yer see, boys, he hed money, and that is about all folks wanter know when a man comes to settle down. And he bought that 'are place, and built that 'are house. He built it all sea-cap'n fashion, so's to feel as much at home as he could. The parlour was like a ship's cabin. The table and chairs was fastened down to the floor, and the closets was made with holes to set the casters and the decanters and bottles in, jest's they be at sea; and there was stanchions to hold on by; and they say that blowy nights the cap'n used to fire up pretty well with his grog, till he hed about all he could carry, and then he'd set and hold on, and hear the wind blow, and kind o' feel out to sea right there to hum. There wasn't no Mis' Cap'n Brown, and there didn't seem likely to be none.

"And whether there ever hed been one, nobody know'd. He hed an old black Guinea nigger-woman, named Quassia, that did his work. She was shaped pretty much like one o' these 'ere great crookneck-squashes. She wa'n't no gret beauty, I can tell you; and she used to wear a gret red turban and a yaller short gown and red petticoat, and a gret string o' gold beads round her neck, and gret big gold hoops in her ears, made right in the middle o' Africa among the heathen there. For all she was black, she thought a heap o' herself, and was consid'able sort o' predominative over the cap'n. Lordy massy! boys, it's allus so.

"Get a man and a woman together—any sort o' woman you're a mind to, don't care who 'tis—and one way or another she gets the rule over him, and he jest has to train to her fife. Some does it one way, and some does it another; some does it by jawin' and some does it by kissin', and some does it by faculty and contrivance; but one way or another they allers does it. Old Cap'n Brown was a good stout, stocky kind o' John Bull sort o' fellow, and a good judge o' sperits. and allers kep' the best in them 'are cupboards o' his'n; but, fust and last, things in his house went pretty much as old Quassia said.

"Folks got to kind o' respectin' Quassia. She come to meetin' Sunday regular, and sot all fixed up in red and yaller and green, with glass beads and what not, lookin' for all the world like one o' them ugly Indian idols; but she was well-behaved as any Christian. She was a master hand at cookin'. Her bread and biscuits couldn't be beat, and no couldn't her pies, and there wa'n't no such pound-cake as she made nowhere. Wal, this 'ere story I'm a goin' to tell you was told me by Cinthy Pendleton. There ain't a more respectable gal, old or young, than Cinthy nowheres. She lives over to Sherburne now, and I hear tell she's sot up a manty-makin' business; but then she used to do tailorin' in Oldtown. She was a member o' the church, and a good Christian as ever was.

"Wal, ye see, Quassia she got Cinthy to come up and spend a week to the Cap'n Brown house, a doin' tailorin' and a fixin' over his close: 'twas along toward the fust o' March. Cinthy she sot by the fire in the front parlour with her goose and her press-board and her work: for there wa'n't no company callin', and the snow was drifted four feet deep right across the front door; so there wa'n't much danger o' anybody comin' in. And the cap'n he was a perlite man to wimmen; and Cinthy she liked it jest as well not to have company, 'cause the cap'n he'd make himself entertainin' tellin' on her sea-stories, and all about his adventures among the Ammonites, and Perresites, and Jebusites, and all sorts o' heathen people he'd been among.

"Wal, that 'are week there come on the master snow-storm. Of all the snowstorms that hed ben, that 'are was the beater; and I tell you the wind blew as if 'twas the last chance it was ever goin' to hev. Wal, it's kind o' scary like to be shet up in a lone house with all natur' a kind o' breakin' out, and goin' on so, and the snow a comin' down so thick ye can't see "cross the street, and the wind a pipin' and a squeelin' and a rumblin' and a tumblin' fust down this chimney and then down that. I tell you, it sort o' sets a feller thinkin' o' the three great things—death, judgment, and etarnaty; and I don't care who the folks is, nor how good they be, there's times when they must be feelin' putty consid'able solemn.

"Wal, Cinthy she said she kind o' felt so along, and she hed a sort o' queer feelin' come over her as if there was somebody or somethin' round the house more'n appeared. She said she sort o' felt it in the air; but it seemed to her silly, and she tried to get over it. But two or three times, she said, when it got to be dusk, she felt somebody go by her up the stairs. The front entry wa'n't very light in the daytime, and in the storm, come five o'clock, it was so dark that all you could see was jest a gleam o' somethin', and two or three times when she started to go upstairs she see a soft white suthin' that seemed goin' up before her, and she stopped with her heart a beatin' like a trip-hammer, and she sort o' saw it go up and along the entry to the cap'n's door, and then

54

it seemed to go right through, 'cause the door didn't open.

"Wal, Cinthy says she to old Quassia, says she, 'Is there anybody lives in this house but us?'

"'Anybody lives here?' says Quassia: 'what you mean?' says she.

"Says Cinthy, 'I thought somebody went past me on the stairs last night and tonight.'

"Lordy massy! how old Quassia did screech and laugh. 'Good Lord!' says she, 'how foolish white folks is! Somebody went past you? Was't the capt'in?'

"'No, it wa'n't the cap'n,' says she: 'it was somethin' soft and white, and moved very still; it was like somethin' in the air,' says she. Then Quassia she haw-hawed louder. Says she, 'It's hysterikes, Miss Cinthy; that's all it is.'

"Wal, Cinthy she was kind o' 'shamed, but for all that she couldn't help herself. Sometimes evenin's she'd be a settin' with the cap'n, and she'd think she'd hear somebody a movin' in his room overhead; and she knowed it wa'n't Quassia, 'cause Quassia was ironin' in the kitchen. She took pains once or twice to find out that 'are.

"Wal, ye see, the cap'n's room was the gret front upper chamber over the parlour, and then right oppisite to it was the gret spare chamber where Cinthy slept. It was jest as grand as could be, with a gret four-post mahogany bedstead and damask curtains brought over from England; but it was cold enough to freeze a white bear solid—the way spare chambers allers is. Then there was the entry between, run straight through the house: one side was old Quassia's room, and the other was a sort o' storeroom, where the old cap'n kep' all sorts o' traps.

"Wal, Cinthy she kep' a hevin' things happen and a seein' things, till she didn't railly know what was in it. Once when she come into the parlour jest at sundown, she was sure she see a white figure a vanishin' out o' the door that went towards the side entry. She said it was so dusk, that all she could see was jest this white figure, and it jest went out still as a cat as she come in.

"Wal, Cinthy didn't like to speak to the cap'n about it. She was a close woman, putty prudent, Cinthy was.

"But one night, 'bout the middle o' the week, this 'ere thing kind o' come to a crisis.

"Cinthy said she'd ben up putty late a sewin' and a finishin' off down in the parlour; and the cap'n he sot up with her, and was consid'able cheerful and entertainin', tellin' her all about things over in the Bermudys, and off to Chiny and Japan, and round the world ginerally. The storm that hed been a blowin' all the week was about as furious as ever; and the cap'n he stirred up a mess o' flip, and hed it for her hot to go to bed on. He was a good-natured critter, and allers had feelin's for lone women; and I s'pose he knew 'twas sort o' desolate for Cinthy.

"Wal, takin' the flip so right the last thing afore goin' to bed, she went right off to sleep as sound as a nut, and slep' on till somewhere about mornin', when she said somethin' waked her broad awake in a minute. Her eyes flew wide open like a spring, and the storm hed gone down and the moon come out; and there, standin' right in the moonlight by her bed, was a woman jest as white as a sheet, with black hair hangin' down to her waist, and the brightest, mourn fullest black eyes you ever see. She stood there lookin' right at Cinthy; and Cinthy thinks that was what waked her up; 'cause, you know, ef anybody stands and looks steady at folks asleep it's apt to wake 'em.

"Anyway, Cinthy said she felt jest as ef she was turnin' to stone. She couldn't move nor speak. She lay a minute, and then she shut her eyes, and begun to say her prayers; and a minute after she opened 'em, and it was gone.

"Cinthy was a sensible gal, and one that allers hed her thoughts about her; and she jest got up and put a shawl round her shoulders, and went first and looked at the doors, and they was both on 'em locked jest as she left 'em when she went to bed. Then she looked under the bed and in the closet, and felt all round the room: where she couldn't see she felt her way, and there wa'n't nothin' there.

"Wal, next mornin' Cinthy got up and went home, and she kep' it to herself a good while. Finally, one day when she was

"*She stood there, lookin' right at Cinthy.*"

workin' to our house she told Hepsy about it, and Hepsy she told me."

"Well, Sam," we said, after a pause, in which we heard only the rustle of leaves and the ticking of branches against each other, "what do you suppose it was?"

"Wal, there 'tis: you know jest as much about it as I do. Hepsy told Cinthy it might 'a' ben a dream; so it might, but Cinthy she was sure it wa'n't a dream, 'cause she remembers plain hearin' the old clock on the stairs strike four while she had her eyes open lookin' at the woman; and then she only shet 'em a minute, jest to say 'Now I lay me,' and opened 'em and she was gone.

"Wal, Cinthy told Hepsy, and Hepsy she kep' it putty close. She didn't tell it to nobody except Aunt Sally Dickerson and the Widder Bije Smith and your Grandma Badger and the minister's wife; and they every one o' 'em 'greed it ought to be kep' close, 'cause it would make talk. Wal, come spring, somehow or other it seemed to 'a' got all over Old-town. I heard on 't to the store and up to the tavern; and Jake Marshall he says to me one day, 'What's this 'ere about the cap'n's house?' And the Widder Loker she says to me, 'There's ben a ghost seen in the cap'n's house;' and I heard on 't clear over to Needham and Sherburne.

"Some o' the women they drew themselves up putty stiff and proper. Your Aunt Lois was one on 'em.

"'Ghost,' says she; 'don't tell me! Perhaps it would be best ef 'twas a ghost,' says she. She didn't think there ought to be no sich doin's in nobody's house; and your grandma she shet her up, and told her she didn't oughter talk so."

"Talk how?" said I, interrupting Sam with wonder. "What did Aunt Lois mean?"

"Why, you see," said Sam mysteriously, "there allers is folks in every town that's jest like the Sadducees in old times: they won't believe in angel nor sperit, no way you can fix it; and ef things is seen and done in a house, why, they say, it's 'cause there's somebody there; there's some sort o' deviltry or trick about it.

"So, the story got round that there was a woman kep' private in Cap'n Brown's house, and that he brought her from furrin parts; and it growed and growed, till there was all sorts o' ways o' tellin on 't.

"Some said they'd seen her a settin' at an open winder. Some said that moonlight nights they'd seen her a walkin' out in the back garden kind o' in and out 'mong the bean-poles and squash-vines.

"You see, it come on spring and summer; and the winders o' the Cap'n Brown house stood open, and folks was all a watchin' on 'em day and night. Aunt Sally Dickerson told the minister's wife that she'd seen in plain daylight a woman a settin' at the chamber winder atween four and five o'clock in the mornin'— jist a settin' a lookin' out and a doin' nothin', like anybody else. She was very white and pale, and had black eyes.

"Some said that it was a nun the cap'n had brought away from a Roman Catholic convent in Spain, and some said he'd got her out o' the Inquisition.

"Aunt Sally said she thought the minister ought to call and inquire why she didn't come to meetin' and who she was, and all about her: 'cause, you see, she said it might be all right enough ef folks only know'd jest how things was; but ef they didn't, why, folks will talk."

"Well, did the minister do it?"

"What, Parson Lothrop? Wal, no, he didn't. He made a call on the cap'n in a regular way, and asked arter his health and all his family. But the cap'n he seemed jest as jolly and chipper as a spring robin, and he gin the minister some o' his old Jamaiky; and the minister he come away and said he didn't see nothin'; and no he didn't. Folks never does see nothin' when they aint' lookin' where 'tis. Fact is, Parson Lothrop wa'n't fond o' inter-ferin'; he was a master hand to slick things over. Your grandma she used to mourn about it, 'cause she said he never gin no p'int to the doctrines; but 'twas all of a piece, he kind o' took every-thing the smooth way.

"But your grandma she believed in the ghost, and so did Lady Lothrop. I was up to her house t'other day fixin' a door-knob, and says she, 'Sam, your wife told me a strange story about the Cap'n Brown house.'

"'Yes, ma'am, she did,' says I.

"'Well, what do you think of it?' says she.

"'Wal, sometimes I think, and then agin I don't know,' says I. 'There's Cinthy she's a member o' the church and a good pious gal,' says I.

"'Yes, Sam,' says Lady Lothrop, says she; 'and Sam,' says she, 'it is jest like something that happened once to my grandmother when she was livin' in the old Province House in Bostin.' Says she, 'These 'ere things is the mysteries of Providence, and it's jest as well not to have 'em too much talked about.'

"'Jest so,' says I—'jest so. That 'are's what every woman I've talked with says; and I guess, fust and last, I've talked with twenty—good, safe church-members—and they's every one o' opinion that this 'ere oughtn't to be talked about. Why, over to the deakin's t'other night we went it all over as much as two or three hours, and we concluded that the best way was to keep quite still about it; and that's jest what they say over to Needham and Sherburne. I've been all round a hushin' this 'ere up, and I hain't found but a few people that hedn't the particulars one way or another.' This 'ere was what I says to Lady Lothrop. The fact was, I never did see no report spread so, nor make sich sort o' sarchin's o' heart, as this 'ere. It railly did beat all; 'cause, ef 'twas a ghost, why there was the p'int proved, ye see.

"Cinthy's a church-member, and she see it, and got right up and sarched the room: but then agin, ef 'twas a woman, why that 'are was kind o' awful; it give cause, ye see, for thinkin' all sorts o' things. There was Cap'n Brown, to be sure, he wa'n't a church-member; but yet he was as honest and regular a man as any goin', as fur as any on us could see. To be sure, nobody know'd where he come from, but that wa'n't no reason agin' him: this 'ere might a ben a crazy sister, or some poor critter that he took out o' the best o' motives; and the Scriptur' says, 'Charity hopeth all things.' But then, ye see, folks will talk,—that 'are's the pester o' all these things,—and they did some on 'em talk consid'able strong about the cap'n; but somehow or other, there didn't nobody come to the p'int o' facin' on him down, and sayin' square out, 'Cap'n Brown, have you got a woman in your house, or hain't you? or is it a ghost, or what is it?' Folks somehow never does come to that. Ye see, there was the cap'n so respectable, a settin' up every Sunday there in his pew, with his ruffles round his hands and his red broadcloth cloak and his cocked hat. Why, folks' hearts sort o' failed 'em when it come to say in' anything right to him. They thought and kind o' whispered round that the minister or the deakins oughter do it: but Lordy massy! ministers, I s'pose, has feelin's like the rest on us; they don't want to eat all the hard cheeses that nobody else won't eat. Anyhow, there wasn't nothin' said direct to the cap'n; and jest for want o' that all the folks in Old-town kep' a bilin' and a bilin' like a kettle o' soap, till it seemed all the time as if they'd bile over.

"Some o' the wimmen tried to get somethin' out o' Quassy. Lordy massy! you might as well 'a' tried to get it out an old tom-turkey, that'll strut and gobble and quitter, and drag his wings on the ground, and fly at you, but won't say nothin'. Quassy she screeched her queer sort o' laugh; and she told 'em that they was a makin' fools o' themselves, and that the cap'n's matters wa'n't none o' their bisness; and that was true enough. As to goin' into Quassia's room, or into any o' the store-rooms or closets she kep' the keys of, you might as well hev gone into a lion's den. She kep' all her places locked up tight; and there was no gettin' at nothin' in the Cap'n Brown house, else I believe some o' the wimmen would 'a' sent a sarch-warrant."

"Well," said I, "what came of it? Didn't anybody ever find out?"

"Wal," said Sam, "it come to an end sort o', and didn't come to an end. It was jest this 'ere way. You see, along in October, jest in the cider-makin' time, Abel Flint he was took down with dysentery and died. You 'member the Flint house: it stood on a little rise o' ground jest lookin' over towards the Brown house. Wal, there was Aunt Sally Dickerson and the Widder Bije Smith, they set up with the corpse. He was laid out in the back chamber, you see, over the milk-room and kitchen; but there was cold victuals and sich in the front chamber, where the watchers sot. Wal, now, Aunt Sally she told me that between three and four o'clock she heard wheels a rumblin', and she went to the winder, and it was clear starlight; and she see a coach come up to the Cap'n Brown house; and she see the cap'n come out bringin' a woman all wrapped in a cloak, and old Quassy came arter with her arms full o' bundles; and he put her into the kerridge, and shet her in, and it driv off; and she see old Quassy stand lookin' over the fence arter it. She tried to wake up the widder, but 'twas towards mornin', and the widder allers was a hard sleeper; so there wa'n't no witness but her.'

"Well, then, it wasn't a ghost," said I, "after all, and it was a woman."

"Wal, there 'tis, you see. Folks don't know that 'are yit, 'cause there it's jest as broad as 'tis long. Now, look at it. There's Cinthy, she's a good, pious gal: she locks her chamber-doors, both on 'em, and goes to bed, and wakes up in the night, and there's a woman there. She jest shets her eyes, and the woman's gone. She gits up and looks, and both doors is locked jest as she left 'em. That 'ere woman wa'n't flesh and blood now, no way—not such flesh and blood as we knows on; but then they say Cinthy might hev dreamed it!

"Wal, now, look at it t'other way. There's Aunt Sally Dickerson; she's a good woman and a church-member: wal, she sees a woman in a cloak with all her bundles brought out o' Cap'n Brown's house, and put into a kerridge, and driv off, atween three and four o'clock in the mornin'. Wal, that 'ere shows there must 'a' ben a real live woman kep' there privately, and so what Cinthy saw wasn't a ghost.

"Wal, now, Cinthy says Aunt Sally might 'a' dreamed it,—that she got her head so full o' stories about the Cap'n Brown house, and watched it till she got asleep, and hed this 'ere dream; and, as there didn't nobody else see it, it might 'a' ben, you know. Aunt Sally's clear she didn't dream, and then agin Cinthy's clear she didn't dream; but which on 'em was awake, or which on 'em was asleep, is what ain't settled in Oldtown yet."

How to Fight the Devil

"Look here, boys," said Sam, "don't you want to go with me up to the Devil's Den this arternoon?"

"Where is the Devil's Den?" said I, with a little awe.

"Wal, it's a longer tramp than I've ever took ye. It's clear up past the pickerel pond, and beyond old Skunk John's pasture-lot. It's a 'mazin' good place for raspberries. shouldn't wonder if we should get two three quarts there. Great rocks there higher 'n yer head; kinder solemn, 'tis."

This was a delightful and seductive account, and we arranged for a walk that very afternoon.

In almost every New-England village the personality of Satan has been acknowledged by calling by his name some particular rock or cave, or other natural object whose singularity would seem to suggest a more than mortal occupancy. "The Devil's Punchbowl," "The Devil's Wash-bowl," "The Devil's Kettle," "The Devil's Pulpit," and "The Devil's Den," have been designations that marked places or objects of some striking natural peculiarity. Often these are found in the midst of the most beautiful and romance scenery, and the sinister name seems to have no effect in lessening its attractions. To me, the very idea of going to the Devil's Den was full of a pleasing horror.

When a boy, I always lived in the shadowy edge of that line which divides spirit land from mortal life, and it was my delight to walk among its half lights and shadows. The old graveyard where, side by side, mouldered the remains of Indian *sachems* and the ancients of English blood, was my favourite haunt. I loved to sit on the graves while the evening mists arose from them, and to fancy cloudy forms waving and beckoning. To me, this spirit land was my only refuge from the dry details of a hard, prosaic life. The schoolroom—with its hard seats rudely fashioned from slabs of rough wood, with its clumsy desks, hacked and ink-stained, with its unintelligible textbooks and its unsympathetic teacher—was to me a prison out of whose weary windows I watched the pomp and glory of nature,—the free birds singing, the clouds sailing, the trees waving and whispering, and longed, as earnestly as ever did the Psalmist, to flee far away, and wander in the wilderness.

Hence, no joy of after life—nothing that the world has now to give—can equal that joyous sense of freedom and full posses-sion which came over me on Saturday afternoons, when I start-ed off on a tramp with the world all before me,—the mighty, unexplored world of mysteries and possibilities, bounded only by the horizon. Ignorant alike of all science, neither botanist nor naturalist, I was studying at first-hand all that lore out of which science is made. Every plant and flower had a familiar face to me, and said something to my imagination. I knew where each was to be found, its time of coming and going, and met them year after year as returning friends.

So, it was with joyous freedom that we boys rambled off with Sam this afternoon, intent to find the Devil's Den. It was a ledge of granite rocks rising in the midst of a grove of pines and white birches. The ground was yellow and slippery with the fallen needles of the pines of other days, and the glistening white stems of the birches shone through the shadows like ivory pillars. Underneath the great granite ledges, all sorts of roots and plants grappled and kept foothold; and whole armies of wild raspberries matured their fruit, rounder and juicier for growing in the shade.

In one place yawned a great rift, or cavern, as if the rocks had been violently twisted and wrenched apart, and a mighty bowlder lodging in the rift had roofed it over, making a cavern of most seductive darkness and depth. This was the Devil's Den;

and after we had picked our pail full of berries, we sat down there to rest.

"Sam, do you suppose the Devil ever was here?" said I. "What do they call this his den for?"

"Massy, child! that 'are was in old witch times. There used to be witch meetins' held here, and awful doins'; they used to have witch sabba' days and witch sacraments, and sell their souls to the old boy."

"What should they want to do that for?"

"Wal, sure enough; what was it for? I can't make out that the Devil ever gin 'em anything, any on 'em. They warn't no richer, nor didn't get no more 'n this world than the rest; and they was took and hung; and then ef they went to torment after that, they hed a pretty bad bargain on't, I say."

"Well, people don't do such things any more, do they?" said I.

"No," said Sam. "Since the gret fuss and row-de-dow about it, it's kind o' died out; but there's those, I s'pose, that hez dealins' with the old boy. Folks du say that old Ketury was a witch, and that, ef 't ben in old times, she'd a hed her neck stretched; but she lived and died in peace."

"But do you think," said I, now proposing the question that lay nearest my heart, "that the Devil can hurt us?"

"That depends consid'able on how you take him," said Sam. "Ye see, come to a straight out-an'-out fight with him, he'll git the better on yer."

"But," said I, "Christian did fight Apollyon, and got him down too."

I had no more doubt in those days that this was an historic fact than I had of the existence of Romulus and Remus and the wolf.

"Wal, that 'ere warn't jest like real things: they say that 'ere's an allegory. But I'll tell ye how old Sarah Bunganuck fit the Devil, when he 'peared to her. Ye see, old Sarah she was one of the converted Injuns, and a good old critter she was too; worked hard, and got her livin' honest. She made baskets, and she made brooms, and she used to pick young wintergreen and tie it up in bunches, and dig *sassafras* and ginsing to make beer; and she got her a little bit o' land, right alongside o' Old Black Hoss John's white-birch wood-lot.

"Now, I've heerd some o' these 'ere modern ministers that come down from Cambridge college, and are larnt about everything in creation, they say there ain't no devil, and the reason on't is, 'cause there can't be none. These 'ere fellers' is so sort o' green!—they don't mean no harm, but they don't know nothin' about nobody that does. If they'd ha known old Black Hoss John, they'd ha' been putty sure there was a devil. He was jest the Grossest, ugliest critter that ever ye see, and he was ugly jest for the sake o' ugliness.

"He couldn't bear to let the boys pick huckleberries in his paster lots, when he didn't pick 'em himself; and he was allers jawin' me 'cause I would go trout-fishin' in one o' his pasters. Jest ez if the trout that swims warn't the Lord's, and jest ez much mine as his. He grudged every critter everything; and if he'd ha' hed his will and way, every bird would ha' fell down dead that picked up a worm on his grounds. He was jest as nippin' as a black frost. Old Black Hoss didn't git drunk in a regerlar way, like Uncle Eph and Toddy Whitney, and the rest o' them boys. But he jest sot at home, a-soakin' on cider, till he was crosser'n a bear with a sore head. Old Black Hoss hed a special spite agin old Sarah. He said she was an old witch and an old thief, and that she stole things offn his grounds, when everybody knew that she was a regerlar church-member, and as decent an old critter as there was goin'.

"As to her stealin' she didn't do nothin' but pick huckleberries and grapes, and git chesnuts and wannuts, and buttenuts, and them 'ere wild things that's the Lord's, grow on whose land they will, and is free to all. I've hearn 'em tell that, over in the old country, the poor was kept under so, that they couldn't shoot a bird, nor ketch a fish, nor gather no nuts, nor do nothin' to keep' from starvin', 'cause the quality folks they thought they owned everything, 'way down to the middle of the earth and clear up to the stars. We never hed no sech doin's this side of the water, thank the Lord! We've allers been free to have the chesnuts and the wannuts and the grapes and the huckleberries and the straw-berries, ef we could git 'em, and ketch fish when and where we was a mind to. Lordy massy! your grandthur's old Cesar, he used to call the pond his pork-pot. He'd jest go down and throw in a line and ketch his dinner.

"Wal, Old Black Hoss he know'd the law was so, and he couldn't do nothin' agin her by law; but he sarved her out every mean trick he could think of. He used to go and stan' and lean over her garden-gate and jaw at her an hour at a time; but old Sarah she had the Injun in her; she didn't run to talk much: she used to jest keep on with her weedin anc her work, jest's if he warn't there, and that made Old Black Hoss madder'n ever; and he thought he'd try and frighten her off'n the ground, by makin' on her believe he was the Devil. So one time, when he'd been killin' a beef critter, they took off the skin with the horns and all on; and Old Black Hoss he says to Toddy and Eph and Loker, 'You jest come up tonight, and see how I'll frighten old Sarah Bunganuck.'

"Wal, Toddy and Eph and Loker, they hedn't no better to do, and they thought they'd jest go round and see. Ye see 'twas a moonlight night, and old Sarah—she was an industrious crit-ter—she was cuttin' white-birch brush for brooms in the paster-lot. Wal, Old Black Hoss he wrapped the critter's skin round him, with the horns on his head, and come and stood by the fence, and begun to roar and make a noise. Old Sarah she kept right on with her work, cuttin' her brush and pilin' on't up, and jest let him roar. Wal, Old Black Hoss felt putty foolish, 'specially ez the fellers were waitin' to see how she took it. So he calls out in a grum voice,—

"'Woman, don't yer know who I be?"

"'No,' says she quite quiet, 'I don't know who yer be.'

"'Wal, I'm the Devil,' sez he.

"'Ye be?' says old Sarah. 'Poor old critter, how I pity ye!' and she never gin him another word, but jest bundled up her broom-stuff, and took it on her back and walked off, and Old Black

" Wal, I'm the Devil, sez he."

Hoss he stood there mighty foolish with his skin and horns; and so he had the laugh agin him, 'cause Eph and Loker they went and told the story down to the tavern, and he felt awful cheap to think old Sarah had got the upper hands on him.

"Wal, ye see, boys, that 'ere's jest the way to fight the Devil. Jest keep straight on with what ye're doin', and don't ye mind him, and he can't do nothin' to ye."

Tom Toothacre's Ghost Story

"What is it about that old house in Sherbourne?" said Aunt Nabby to Sam Lawson, as he sat drooping over the coals of a great fire one October evening.

Aunt Lois was gone to Boston on a visit; and, the smart spice of her scepticism being absent, we felt fine more freedom to start our story-teller on one of his legends.

Aunt Nabby sat trotting her knitting-needles on a blue-mixed yarn stocking. Grandmamma was knitting in unison at the other side of the fire, Grandfather sat studying *The Boston Courier*. The wind outside was sighing in fitful wails, creaking the pantry-doors, occasionally puffing in a vicious gust down the broad throat of the chimney. It was a drizzly, sleety evening; and the wet lilac-bushes now and then rattled and splashed against the window as the wind moaned and whispered through them.

We boys had made preparation for a comfortable evening. We had enticed Sam to the chimney-corner, and drawn him a mug of cider. We had set down a row of apples to roast on the hearth, which even now were giving faint sighs and sputters as their plump sides burst in the genial heat. The big oak back-log simmered and bubbled, and distilled large drops down amid the ashes; and the great hickory forestick had just burned out into solid bright coals, faintly skimmed over with white ashes. The whole area of the big chimney was full of a sleepy warmth and brightness just calculated to call forth fancies and visions. It only wanted somebody now to set Sam off; and Aunt Nabby broached the ever-interesting subject of haunted houses.

"Wal, now, Miss Badger," said Sam, "I ben over there, and walked round that 'are house consid'able; and I talked with Granny Hokum and Aunt Polly, and they've putty much come to the conclusion that they'll hev to move out on't. Ye see these 'ere noises, they keep 'em awake nights; and Aunt Polly, she gets 'stericky; and Hannah Jane, she says, ef they stay in the house, she can't live with 'em no longer. And what can them lone women do without Hannah Jane? Why, Hannah Jane, she says these two months past she's seen a woman, regular, walking up and down the front hall between twelve and one o'clock at night; and it's jist the image and body of old Ma'am Tillotson, Parson Ho-kum's mother, that everybody know'd was a thunderin' land o' woman, that kep' everything in a muss while she was alive.

"What the old crittur's up to now there ain't no knowin'. Some folks seems to think it's a sign Granny Hokum's time's comin'. But Lordy massy! says she to me, says she, 'Why, Sam, I don't know nothin' what I've done, that Ma'am Tillotson should be set loose on me.' Anyway, they've all got so narvy, that Jed Hokum has ben up from Needham, and is goin' to cart 'em all over to live with him. Jed, he's for hushin' on't up, 'cause he says it brings a bad name on the property.

"Wal, I talked with Jed about it; and says I to Jed, says I, 'Now, ef you'll take my advice, jist you give that 'are old house a regu-lar overhaulin', and paint it over with tew coats o' paint, and that are'll clear 'em out, if any thing will. Ghosts is like bedbugs,—they can't stan' fresh paint,' says I. 'They allers clear out. I've seen it tried on a ship that got haunted.'"

"Why, Sam, do ships get haunted?"

"To be sure they do!—haunted the wust kind. Why, I could tell ye a story'd make your har rise on e'end, only I'm 'fraid of frightening boys when they're jist going to bed."

"Oh! you can't frighten Horace," said my grandmother. "He will go and sit out there in the graveyard till nine o'clock nights, spite of all I tell him."

"Do tell, Sam!" we urged. "What was it about the ship?"

Sam lifted his mug of cider, deliberately turned it round and round in his hands, eyed it affectionately, took a long drink, and set it down in front of him on the hearth, and began:—

"Ye 'member I told you how I went to sea down East, when I was a boy, 'long with Tom Toothacre. Wal, Tom, he reeled off a yarn one night that was 'bout the toughest I ever hed the pullin' on. And it come all straight, too, from Tom. 'Twa'n't none o' yer hearsay: 'twas what he seen with his own eyes. Now, there wa'n't no nonsense 'bout Tom, not a bit on't; and he wa'n't afeard o' the divil himse'f; and he ginally saw through things about as straight as things could be seen through. This 'ere happened when Tom was mate o' *The Albatross*, and they was a-runnin' up to the Banks for a fare o' fish. *The Albatross* was as handsome a craft as ever ye see; and Cap'n Sim Withespoon, he was skipper—a rail nice likely man he was. I heard Tom tell this 'ere one night to the boys on *The Brilliant*, when they was all a-settin round the stove in the cabin one foggy night that we was to anchor in Frenchman's Bay, and all kind o' layin' off loose.

"Tom, he said they was having a famous run up to the Banks. There was a spankin' southerly, that blew 'em along like all natur'; and they was hevin' the best kind of a time, when this 'ere southerly brought a pesky fog down on 'em, and it grew thicker than hasty-puddin'. Ye see, that 'are's the pester o' these 'ere southerlies: they's the biggest fog-breeders there is goin'. And so, putty soon, you couldn't see half ship's length afore you.

"Wal, they all was down to supper, except Dan Sawyer at the wheel, when there come sich a crash as if heaven and earth was a-splittin', and then a scrapin' and thump bumpin' under the ship, and gin 'em sich a h'ist that the pot o' beans went rollin', and brought up jam ag'in the bulk-head; and the fellers was keeled over,—men and pork and beans kinder permiscus.

"'The divil!' says Tom Toothacre, 'we've run down somebody. Look out, up there!'

"Dan, he shoved the helm hard down, and put her up to the wind, and sung out, 'Lordy massy! we've struck her right amidships!'

73

"'Struck what?' they all yelled, and tumbled up on deck.

"'Why, a little schooner,' says Dan. 'Didn't see her till we was right on her. She's gone down tack and sheet. Look! there's part o' the wreck a-floating off: don't ye see?'

"Wal, they didn't see, 'cause it was so thick you couldn't hardly see your hand afore your face. But they put about, and sent out a boat, and land o' sarched round; but, Lordy massy! ye might as well looked for a drop of water in the Atlantic Ocean. Whoever they was, it was all done gone and over with 'em for this life, poor critturs!

"Tom says they felt confoundedly about it; but what could they do? Lordy massy! what can any on us do? There's places where folks jest lets go 'cause they hes to, Things ain't as they want 'em, and they can't alter 'em. Sailors ain't so rough as they look: they'z feelin' critturs, come to put things right to 'em. And there wasn't one on 'em who wouldn't 'a' worked all night for a chance o' saving sime o' them poor fellows. But there 'twas, and twa'n't no use trying.

"Wal, so they sailed on; and by'm by the wind kind o' chopped round no'theast, and then come round east, and sot in for one of them regular east blows and drizzles that takes the starch out o' fellers more'n a regular storm. So, they concluded they might as well put into a little bay there, and come to anchor.

"So, they sot an anchor-watch, and all turned in.

"Wal, now comes the particular curus part o' Tom's story; and it was more curus 'cause Tom was one that wouldn't 'a' believed no other man that had told it. Tom was one o' your sort of philosophers. He was fer lookin' into things, and wa'n't in no hurry 'bout believin'; so that this 'un was more 'markable on account of it's bein' Tom that seen it than ef it had ben others.

"Tom says that night he hed a pesky toothache that sort o' kep' grumblin' and jumpin' so he couldn't go to sleep; and he lay in his bunk, a-turnin' this way and that, till long past twelve o'clock.

"Tom had a 'thwart-ship bunk where he could see into every bunk on board, except Bob Coffin's; and Bob was on the anchor-watch. Wal, he lay there, tryin' to go to sleep, hearin' the men snorin like bull-frogs in a swamp, and watchin' the lantern a-swingin' back and forward; and the sou'westers and pea-jackets were kinder throwin' their long shadders up and down as the vessel sort o' rolled and pitched,—for there was a heavy swell on,—and then he'd hear Bob Coffin *tramp, tramp, trampin'* overhead,—for Bob had a pretty heavy foot of his own,—and all sort o' mixed up together with Tom's toothache, so he couldn't get to sleep. Finally, Tom, he bit off a great chaw o' 'baccy, and got it well sot in his cheek, and kind o' turned over to lie on't, and ease the pain. Wal, he says he laid a spell, and dropped off in a sort o' doze, when he woke in sich a chill his teeth chattered, and the pain come on like a knife, and he bounced over, thinking the fire had gone out in the stove.

"Wal, sure enough, he see a man a-crouchin' over the stove, with his back to him, a-stretchin' out his hands to warm 'em. He had on a sou'wester and a pea-jacket, with a red tippet round his neck; and his clothes was drippin' as if he'd just come in from a rain.

"'What the divil!' says Tom. And he riz right up, and rubbed his eyes. 'Bill Bridges,' says he, 'what shine be you up to now?' For Bill was a master oneasy crittur, and allers a-gettin' up and walkin' nights; and Tom, he thought it was Bill. But in a minute, he looked over, and there, sure enough, was Bill, fast asleep in his bunk, mouth wide open, snoring like a Jericho ram's-horn. Tom looked round, and counted every man in his bunk, and then says he, 'Who the devil is this? for there's Bob Coffin on deck, and the rest is all here.'

"Wal, Tom wa'n't a man to be put under too easy. He hed his thoughts about him allers; and the fust he thought in every pinch was what to do. So, he sot considerin' a minute, sort o' winkin' his eyes to be sure he saw straight, when, sure enough, there come another man backin' down the companion-way.

"'Wal, there's Bob Coffin, anyhow,' says Tom to himself. But no, the other man, he turned: Tom see his face; and, sure as you live, it was the face of a dead corpse. Its eyes was sot, and it jest came as still across the cabin, and sot down by the stove, and kind o' shivered, and put out its hands as if it was gettin' warm.

"Tom said that there was a cold air round in the cabin, as if an iceberg was comin' near, and he felt cold chills running down his back; but he jumped out of his bunk, and took a step forward. 'Speak!' says he. 'Who be you? and what do you want?'

"They never spoke, nor looked up, but kept kind o' shivering and crouching over the stove.

"'Wal,' says Tom, 'I'll see who you be, anyhow.' And he walked right up to the last man that come in, and reached out to catch hold of his coat-collar; but his hand jest went through him like moonshine, and in a minute he all faded away; and when he turned round the other one was gone too. Tom stood there, looking this way and that; but there warn't nothing but the old stove, and the lantern swingin', and the men all snorin' round in their bunks. Tom, he sung out to Bob Coffin. 'Hullo, up there!' says he. But Bob never answered, and Tom, he went up, and found Bob down on his knees, his teeth a-chatterin' like a bag o' nails, trying to say his prayers; and all he could think of was, 'Now I lay me,' and he kep' going that over and over. Ye see, boys, Bob was a drefful wicked, swearin' crittur, and hadn't said no prayers since he was tew years old, and it didn't come natural to him. Tom give a grip on his collar, and shook him. 'Hold yer yawp,' said he. 'What you howlin' about? What's up?'

"'Oh, Lordy massy' says Bob, 'we're sent for,—all on us,—there's been two on 'em: both on 'em went right by me!'

"Wal, Tom, he hed his own thoughts; but he was bound to get to the bottom of things, anyway. Ef 'twas the devil, well and good—he wanted to know it. Tom jest wanted to hev the matter settled one way or t'other: so, he got Bob sort o' stroked down, and made him tell what he saw.

"Bob, he stood to it that he was a-standin' right for'ard, a-leanin' on the windlass, and kind o' hummin' a tune, when he looked down, and see a sort o' queer light in the fog; and he went and took a look over the bows, when up came a man's head in a sort of sou'wester, and then a pair of hands, and catched at the bob-stay; and then the full figger of a man riz right out o' the water, and clim up on the martingale till he could reach the jib-stay with his hands, and then he swung himself right up onto the bowsprit, and stepped aboard, and went past Bob, right aft, and down into the cabin. And he hadn't more'n got down, afore he turned round, and there was another comin' in over the bowsprit, and he went by him, and down below: so, there was two on 'em, jest as Tom had seen in the cabin.

"Tom he studied on it a spell, and finally says he, 'Bob, let you and me keep this 'ere to ouselves, and see ef it'll come again. Ef it don't, well and good: ef it does—why, we'll see about it.'

"But Tom he told Cap'n Witherspoon, and the cap'n he agreed to keep an eye out the next night. But there warn't nothing said to the rest o' the men.

"Wal, the next night they put Bill Bridges on the watch. The fog had lifted, and they had a fair wind, and was going on steady. The men all turned in, and went fast asleep, except Cap'n Witherspoon, Tom, and Bob Coffin. Wal, sure enough, 'twixt twelve and one o'clock, the same thing came over, only there war four men 'stead o' two. They come in jes' so over the bowsprit, and they looked neither to right nor left, but clim downstairs, and sot down, and crouched and shivered over the stove jist like the others. Wal, Bill Bridges, he came tearin' down like a wild-cat, frightened half out o' his wits, screechin' 'Lord, have mercy! we're all goin' to the devil!' And then they all vanished.

"'Now, Cap'n, what's to be done?' says Tom. 'Ef these 'ere fellows is to take passage, we can't do nothin' with the boys: that's clear.'

"Wal, so it turned out; for, come next night, there was six on 'em come in, and the story got round, and the boys was all on eend. There wa'n't no doin' nothin' with 'em. Ye see, it's allers jest so. Not but what dead folks is jest as 'spectable as they was afore they's dead. These might 'a' been as good fellers as any aboard; but it's human natur'. The minute a feller's dead, why, you sort o' don't know 'bout him; and it's kind o' skeery hevin' on him round; and so 'twan't no wonder the boys didn't feel as if they could go on with the vy'ge, ef these 'ere fellers was all to take passage. Come to look, too, there war consid'able of a leak stove in the vessel; and the boys, they all stood to it, ef they went farther, that they'd all go to the bottom. For, ye see, once the story got a-goin', every one on 'em saw a new thing, every night. One on 'em saw the bait-mill a-grindin', without no hands to grind it; and another saw fellers up aloft, workin' in the sails. Wal, the fact war, they jest had to put about,—run back to Castine.

"Wal, the owners, they hushed up things the best they could; and they put the vessel on the stocks, and worked her over, and put a new coat o' paint on her, and called her *The Betsey Ann*; and she went a good vy'ge to the Banks, and brought home the biggest fare o' fish that had been for a long time; and she's made good vy'ges ever since; and that jest proves what I've been a-saying,—that there's nothin' to drive out ghosts like fresh paint."

A Student's Sea Story

Among the pleasantest of my recollections of old Bowdoin is the salt-air flavour of its sea experiences. The site of Brunswick is a sandy plain, on which the college buildings seem to have been dropped for the good old Yankee economic reason of using land for public buddings that could not be used for anything else. The soil was a fathomless depth of dry, sharp, barren sand, out of whose bosom nothing but pitch-pines and blueberry-bushes emerged, or ever could emerge without superhuman efforts of cultivation.

But these sandy plains, these pine forests, were neighbours to the great, lively, musical blue ocean, whose life-giving presence made itself seen, heard, and felt every hour of the day and night. The beautiful peculiarity of the Maine coast, where the sea interpenetrates the land in pictuesque fiords and lakes, brought a constant romantic element into the landscape.

White-winged ships from India or China came gliding into the lonely solitude of forest recesses, bringing news from strange lands, and tidings of wild adventure, into secluded farmhouses, that, for the most part, seemed to be dreaming in woodland solitude. In the early days of my college life the shipping interest of Maine gave it an outlook into all the countries of the earth. Ships and ship-building and ship-launching were the drift of the popular thought; and the very minds of the people by this commerce had apparently

Suffered a sea change
Into something rare and strange.

There was a quaintness, shrewdness, and vivacity about these men, half skipper, half farmer, that was piquant and enlivening.

It was in the auspicious period of approaching Thanksgiving that my chum and I resolved to antedate for a few days our vacation, and take passage on the little sloop *Brilliant*, that lay curtseying and teetering on the bright waters of Maquoit Bay, loading up to make her Thanksgiving trip to Boston.

It was a bright Indian-summer afternoon that saw us all on board the little craft. She was laden deep with dainties and rarities for the festal appetites of Boston *nabobs*,—loads of those mealy potatoes for which the fields of Maine were justly famed, barrels of ruby cranberries, boxes of solid golden butter (ventures of a thrifty housemother emulous to gather kindred gold in the Boston market). Then there were dressed chickens, turkeys, and geese, all going the same way, on the same errand; and there were sides and saddles of that choice mutton for which the sea islands of Maine were as famous as the South Downs of England.

Everything in such a stowage was suggestive of good cheer. The little craft itself had a sociable, friendly, domestic air. The captain and mate were cousins: the men were all neighbours, sons of families who had grown up together. There was a kindly home flavour in the very stowage of the cargo. Here were Melissa's cranberries, and by many a joke and wink we were apprised that the mate had a tender interest in that venture. There was Widder Toothacre's butter, concerning which there were various comments and speculations, but which was handled and cared for with the consideration the Maine sailor-boy always gives to "the widder."

There was a private keg of very choice eggs, over which the name of Lucindy Ann was breathed by a bright-eyed, lively youngster, who had promised to bring her back the change, and as to the precise particulars of this change many a witticism was expended.

Our mode of living on the *Brilliant* was of the simplest and most primitive kind. On each side the staircase that led down to the cabin, hooped strongly to the partition, was a barrel, which on the one side contained salt beef, and or the other salt pork. A piece out of each barrel, delivered regularly to the cook, formed the foundation of our daily meals; and sea-biscuit and potatoes, with the sauce of salt-water appetites, made this a feast for a king. I make no mention here of gingerbread and doughnuts, and such like ornamental accessories, which were not wanting, nor of nuts and sweet cider, which were to be had for the asking. At meal-times a swing-shelf, which at other seasons hung flat against the wall, was propped up, and our meals were eaten thereon in joyous satisfaction.

A joyous, rollicking set we were, and the whole expedition was a frolic of the first water. One of the drollest features of these little impromptu voyages often was the woe-begone aspect of some unsuspecting land-lubber, who had been beguiled into thinking that he would like a trip to Boston by seeing the pretty *Brilliant* curtseying in the smooth waters of Maquoit, and so had embarked, in innocent ignorance of the physiological results of such enterprises.

I remember the first morning out. As we were driving ahead, under a stiff breeze, I came on deck, and found the respectable Deacon Muggins, who in his Sunday coat had serenely embarked the day before, now desolately clinging to the railing, very white about the gills, and contemplating the sea with a most suggestive expression of disgust and horror.

"Why, deacon, good-morning! How are you? Splendid morning!" said I maliciously.

He drew a deep breath, surveyed me with a mixture of indignation and despair, and then gave vent to his feelings: "Tell ye what: there was one darned old fool up to Brunswick yesterday! but he ain't there now: he's here." The deacon, in the weekly prayer-meeting at Brunswick, used to talk of the necessity of being "emptied of self:" he seemed to be in the way of it in the most literal manner at the present moment. In a few minutes he was extended on the deck, the most utterly limp and dejected of deacons, and vowing with energy, if he ever got out o' this 'ere, you wouldn't catch him again. Of course, my chum and I were not seasick. We were prosperous young sophomores in Bowdoin College and would have scorned to acknowledge suck a weakness. In fact, we were in that happy state of self-opinion where we surveyed everything in creation, as birds do, from above, and were disposed to patronise everybody we met, with a pleasing conviction that there was nothing worth knowing, but what we were likely to know, or worth doing, but what we could do.

Capt. Stanwood liked us, and we liked him: we patronised him, and he was quietly amused at our patronage, and returned it in kind. He was a good specimen of the sea-captain in those early days in Maine: a man in middle life, tall, thin, wiry, and active, full of resource and shrewd mother-wit; a man very confident in his opinions, because his knowledge was all got at first-hand,— the result of a careful use of his own five senses. From his childhood he had followed the seas, and, as he grew older, made voyages to Archangel, to Messina, to the West Indies, and finally round the Horn; and, having carried a very sharp and careful pair of eyes, he had acquired not only a snug competency of worldly goods, but a large stock of facts and inductions, which stood him instead of an education.

He was master of a thriving farm at Harpswell, and, being tethered somewhat by love of wife and children, was mostly stationary there, yet solaced himself by running a little schooner to Boston, and driving a thriving bit of trade by the means. With that reverence for learning which never deserts the New-Englander, he liked us the better for being collegians, and amiably conceded that there were things quite worth knowing taught "up to Brunswick there," though he delighted now and then to show his superiority in talking about what he knew better than we.

Jim Larned, the mate, was a lusty youngster, a sister's son whom he had taken in training in the way he should go. Jim had already made a voyage to Liverpool and the East Indies, and felt himself also quite an authority in his own way.

The evenings were raw and cool; and we generally gathered

round the cabin stove, cracking walnuts, smoking, and telling stories, and having a jolly time generally. It is but due to those old days to say that a most respectable Puritan flavour penetrated even the recesses of those coasters—a sort of gentle Bible and psalm-book aroma, so that there was not a word or a joke among the men to annoy the susceptibilities even of a deacon. Our deacon, somewhat consoled and amended, lay serene in his berth, rather enjoying the yarns that we were spinning. The web, of course, was many-coloured—of quaint and strange and wonderful; and, as the night wore on, it was dyed in certain weird tints of the supernatural.

"Well," said Jim Larned, "folks may say what they're a mind to: there are things that there's no sort o' way o' 'countin' for— things you've jist got to say. Well, here's suthin' to work that I don't know nothin' about; and, come to question any man up sharp, you'll find he's seen one thing o' that sort himself; and this 'ere I'm going to tell's *my* story:—

"Four years ago, I went down to Aunt Jerushy's at Fair Haven. Her husband's in the oysterin' business, and I used to go out with him considerable. Well, there was Bill Jones there—a real bright fellow, one of your open-handed, lively fellows—and he took a fancy to me, and I to him, and he and I stuck up a friendship. He run an oyster-smack to New York, and did a considerable good business for a young man. Well, Bill had a fellow on his smack that I never liked the looks of. He was from the Malays, or some foeign crittur, or other; spoke broken English; had eyes set kind o' edgeways 'n his head: homely as sin he was, and I always mistrusted him.

"'Bill,' I used to say, 'you look out for that fellow: don't you trust him. If I was you, I'd ship him off short metre.' But Bill, he only laughed. 'Why,' says he, 'I can get double work for the same pay out o' that fellow; and what do I care if he ain't handsome?' I remember how chipper an' cheery Bill looked when he was sayin' that, just as he was going down to New York with his load o' oysters. Well, the next night I was sound asleep in Aunt Jerusha's front-chamber that opens towards the Sound, and I was waked right clear out o' sleep by Bill's voice screaming to me.

I got up and run to the window, and looked out, and I heard it again, plain as anything: 'Jim, Jim, Help, help!' It wasn't a common cry, neither: it was screeched out, as if somebody was murdering him. I tell you, it rung through my head for weeks afterwards."

"Well, what came of it?" said my chum, as the narrator made a pause, and we all looked at him in silence.

"Well, as nigh as we can make it out, that very night poor Bill *was* murdered by that very Malay feller: leastways, his body was found in his boat. He'd been stabbed, and all his money and watch and things taken, and this Malay was gone nobody knew where. That's all that was ever known about it."

"But surely," said my chum, who was of a very literal and rationalistic turn of mind, "it couldn't have been his voice you heard: he must have been down to the other end of the Sound, close by New York, by that time."

"Well," said the mate, "all I know is, that I was waked out of sleep by Bill's voice calling my name, screaming in a real agony. It went through me like lightning; and then I find he was murdered that night. Now, I don't know anything about it. I know I heard him calling me; I know he was murdered: but *how* it was, or *what* it was, or *why* it was, I don't know."

"These 'ere college boys can tell ye," said the captain. "Of course, they've got into sophomore year, and there ain't nothing in heaven or earth that they don't know."

"No," said I, "I say with Hamlet, 'There are more things in heaven and earth, Horatio, than are dreamed of in your philosophy.'"

"Well," said my chum, with the air of a philosopher, "what shakes my faith in all supernatural stories is, that I can't see any use or purpose in them."

"Wal, if there couldn't nothin' happen nor be except what *you* could see a use in, there wouldn't *much* happen nor be," quoth the captain.

A laugh went round at the expense of my friend.

"Wal, now, I'll tell ye what, boys," piped the thin voice of the deacon, "folks mustn't be too presumptuous: there is providences permitted that we don't see no use in; but they do happen—yes, they do. Now, what Jim Larned's been a-tellin' is a good deal like what happened to me once, when I was up to Umbagog, in the lumberin' business."

"Halloo!" called out Jim, "here's the deacon's story! I told you every man had one.—Give it to us, deacon! Speak out, and don't be bashful!"

"Wal, really, it ain't what I like to talk about," said the deacon, in a quavering, uncertain voice; "but I don't know but I may as well, though.

"It was that winter I was up to Umbagog. I was clerk, and kep' the 'counts and books, and all that; and Tom Huly,—he was surveyor and marker,—he was there with me, and we chummed together. And there was Jack Cutter; he was jest out o' college: he was there practising surveyin' with him. We three had a kind o' pine-board sort o' shanty, built out on a plain near by the camp: it had a fireplace, and two windows, and our bunks, and each of us had our tables and books and things.

"Well, Huly, he started with a party of three or four to go up through the woods to look out a new tract. It was two or three days' journey through the woods; and jest about that time the Indians up there was getting sort o' uneasy, and we all thought mabbe 'twas sort o' risky: howsomdever, Tom had gone off in high spirits, and told us to be sure and take care of his books and papers. Tom had a lot of books, and thought everything of 'em, and was sort o' particular and nice about his papers. His table sot up one side, by the winder, where he could see to read and write. Well, he'd been gone four days, when one night—it was a bright moonlight night—Jack and I were sitting by the fire, reading, and between nine and ten o'clock there came a strong, regular knock on the window over by Tom's table. We were sitting with our backs to the window. 'Halloo!' says Jack, 'who's that?' We both jumped up, and went to the window and looked out, and see there warn't nobody there.

"'This is curus,' said I.

"'Some of the boys trying to trick us,' says he. 'Let's keep watch: perhaps they'll do it again,' says he.

"We sot down by the fire, and 'fore long it came again.

"Then Jack and I both cut out the door, and run round the house—he one way, and I the other. It was light as day, and nothin' for anybody to hide behind, and there warn't a critter in sight. Well, we come in and sot down, and looked at each other kind o' puzzled, when it come agin, harder'n ever; and Jack looked to the window, and got as white as a sheet.

"'For the Lord's sake, do look!' says he. And you may believe me or not; but I tell you it's a solemn fact: Tom's books was movin',—jest as if somebody was pickin' 'em up, and putting 'em down again, jest as I've seen him do a hundred times.

"'Jack,' says I, 'something's happened to Tom.'

"Wal, there had. That very night Tom was murdered by the Indians. We put down the date, and a week arter the news came."

"Come now, captain," said I, breaking the pause that followed the deacon's story, "give us your story. You've been all over the world, in all times and all weathers, and you ain't a man to be taken in. Did you ever see anything of this sort?"

"Well, now, boys, since you put it straight at me, I don't care if I say I have—on these 'ere very waters we're a-sailin' over now, on board this very schooner, in this very cabin."

This was bringing matters close home. We felt an agreeable shiver, and looked over our shoulders: the deacon, in his berth, raised up on his elbow, and ejaculated, "Dew tell! ye don't say so!"

"Tell us about it, captain," we both insisted. "We'll take your word for most anything."

"Well, it happened about five years ago. It's goin' on now eight years ago that my father died. He sailed out of Gloucester: had his house there; and, after he died, mother, she jest kep' on in the old place. I went down at first to see her fixed up about right, and after that I went now and then, and now and then I sent money. Well, it was about Thanksgiving time, as it is now, and I'd ben down to Boston, and was coming back pretty well loaded with the things I'd been buying in Boston for Thanksgiving at home,—raisins and sugar, and all sorts of West Ingy goods, for the folks in Harpswell. Well, I meant to have gone down to Gloucester to see mother; but I had so many ways to run, and so much to do, I was afraid I wouldn't be back on time; and so, I didn't see her.

"Well, we was driving back with a good stiff breeze, and we'd got past Cape Ann, and I'd gone down and turned in, and was fast asleep in my berth. It was past midnight: everyone on the schooner asleep, except the mate, who was up on the watch. I was sleepin' as sound as ever I slept in my life—not a dream, nor a feelin', no more'n if I had been dead—when suddenly I waked square up. My eyes flew open like a spring, with my mind clear and wide awake, and, sure as I ever see anything, I see my father standing right in the middle of the cabin, looking right at me. I rose right up in my berth, and says I,—

"'Father, is that you?'

"'Yes,' says he, 'it is me.'

"'Father,' says I, 'what do you come for?'

"'Sam,' says he, 'do you go right back to Gloucester, and take your mother home with you, and keep her there as long as she lives.'

"And says I, 'Father, I will.' And as I said this he faded out and was gone. I got right up, and run up on deck, and called out, ''Bout ship!' Mr. More—he was my mate then—stared at me as if he didn't believe his ears. ''Bout ship!' says I. 'I'm going to Gloucester.'

"Well, he put the ship about, and then came to me, and says, 'What the devil does this mean? We're way past Cape Ann. It's forty miles right back to Gloucester.'

"'Can't help it,' I said. 'To Gloucester I must go as quick as wind and water will carry me. I've thought of matters there that I *must* attend to, no matter what happens.'

"Well, Ben More and I were good friends always; but I tell you all that day he watched me, in a curious kind of way, to see if I weren't took with a fever, or suthin; and the men, they whispered and talked among themselves. You see, they all had their own reasons for wanting to be back to Thanksgiving, and it was hard on 'em.

"Well, it was just about sun up we got into Gloucester, and I went ashore. And there was mother, looking pretty poorly, jest making her fire, and getting on her kettle. When she saw me, she held up her hands, and burst out crying—

"'Why, Sam, the Lord must 'a' sent you! I've ben sick and all alone, having a drefful hard time, and I've felt as if I couldn't hold out much longer.'

"'Well,' says I, 'mother, pack up your things, and come right aboard the sloop; for I've come to take you home, and take care of you: so, put up your things.'

"Well, I took hold and helped her, and we put things together lively, and packed up her trunks, and tied up the bed and pillows and bedclothes, and took her rocking-chair and bureau and tables and chairs down to the sloop. And when I came down, bringing her and all her things, Ben More seemed to see what I was after; but how or why the idea came into my head I never told him. There's things that a man feels shy of tellin', and I didn't want to talk about it.

"Well, when we was all aboard, the wind sprung up fair and steady, and we went on at a right spanking pace; and the fellows said the Harpswell girls had got hold of our rope, and was pulling us with all their might; and we came in all right the very day before Thanksgiving. And my wife was as glad to see mother as if she'd expected her, and fixed up the front-chamber for her, with a stove in't, and plenty of kindlings. And the children was all so glad to see grandma, and we had the best kind of a Thanksgiving!"

"Well," said I, "nobody could say there wasn't any use in *that* spirit's coming (if spirit it was) it had a most practical purpose."

"Well," said the captain, "I've been all round the world, in all sorts of countries, seen all sorts of queer, strange things, and seen so many things that I never could have believed if I hadn't seen 'em, that I never say I won't believe this or that. If I see a thing right straight under my eyes, I don't say it couldn't 'a' ben there 'cause college-folks say there ain't no such things."

"How do you know it wasn't all a dream?" said my chum.

"How do I know? 'Cause I was broad awake, and I gen'lly know when I'm awake and when I'm asleep. I think Mr. More found me pretty wide awake."

It was now time to turn in, and we slept soundly while the *Brilliant* ploughed her way. By daybreak the dome of the State House was in sight.

"I've settled the captain's story," said my chum to me. "It can all be accounted for on the theory of cerebral hallucination."

"All right," said I; "but it answered the purpose beautifully for the old mother."

The Visit to the Haunted House

My story now approaches a point in which I am soon to meet and begin to feel the force of a train of circumstances which ruled and shaped my whole life. That I had been hitherto a somewhat exceptional child may perhaps have been made apparent in the incidents I have narrated. I was not, in fact, in the least like what an average healthy boy ought to be. My brother Bill was exactly that, and nothing more. He was a good, growing, well-limbed, comfortably disposed animal, reasonably docile, and capable, under fair government, of being made to go exactly in any paths his elders chose to mark out for him.

It had been settled, the night after my father's funeral, that my Uncle Jacob was to have him for a farm-boy, to work in the summer on the farm, and to pick up his education as he might at the district school in the winter season; and thus my mother was relieved of the burden of his support, and Aunt Lois of his superfluous activity in our home department. To me the loss was a small one; for except a very slight sympathy of souls in the matter of fish-hooks and popguns, there was scarcely a single feeling that we had in common. I had a perfect passion for books, and he had a solid and well-pronounced horror of them, which seems to belong to the nature of a growing boy.

I could read, as by a kind of preternatural instinct, as soon as I could walk; and reading was with me at ten years a devouring passion. No matter what the book was that was left in my vicinity, I read it as by an irresistible fascination. To be sure, I preferred stories, history, and lively narrative, where such material was to be had; but the passion for reading was like hunger—it must be fed, and, and the absence of palatable food, preyed upon what it could find. So, it came to pass that theological tracts, treatises on agriculture, old sermons—anything, in short, that could be raked out of the barrels and boxes in my grandfather's garret—would hold me absorbed in some shady nook of the house when I ought to have been out playing as a proper boy should.

I did not, of course, understand the half of what I read, and miscalled the words to myself in a way that would have been laughable had anybody heard me but the strange, unknown sounds stimulated vague and dreamy images in my mind, which were continually seething, changing, and interweaving, like fog-wreaths by moonlight, and formed phantasmagoria in which I took a quaint and solemn delight.

But there was one peculiarity of my childhood which I have hesitated with an odd sort of reluctance to speak of, and yet which so powerfully influenced and determined my life, and that of all with whom I was connected, that it must find some place here. I was, as I said, dreamy and imaginative, with a mind full of vague yearnings. But beside that, through an extreme delicacy of nervous organisation, my childish steps were surrounded by a species of vision or apparition so clear and distinct that I often found great difficulty in discriminating between the forms of real life and these shifting shapes, that had every appearance of reality, except that they dissolved at the touch. All my favourite haunts had their particular shapes and forms, which it afforded me infinite amusement to watch in their varying movements.

Particularly at night, after I had gone to bed and the candle was removed from my room, the whole atmosphere around my bed seemed like that which Raphael has shadowed forth around his Madonna San Sisto—a palpitating crowd of faces and forms changing in dim and gliding quietude. I have often wondered whether any personal experience similar to mine suggested to the artist this living background to his picture.

For the most part, these phantasms were agreeable to me, and filled me with a dreamy delight. Sometimes distinct scenes or visions would rise before my mind, in which I seemed to look far beyond the walls of the house, and to see things passing wherein were several actors. I remember one of these, which I saw very often, representing a venerable old white-headed man playing on a violin. He was always accompanied by a tall, majestic woman, dressed in a strange, outlandish costume, in which I particularly remarked a high far cap of a peculiar form. As he played, the woman appeared to dance in time to the music.

Another scene which frequently presented itself to my eyes was that of a green meadow by the side of a lake of very calm water. From a grove on one side of the lake would issue a miniature form of a woman clothed in white, with a wide golden girdle around her waist, and long, black hair hanging down to her middle, which she constantly smoothed down with both her hands, with a gentle, rhythmical movement, as she approached me. At a certain point of approach, she always turned her back, and began a rapid retreat into the grove; and invariably as she turned there appeared behind her the image of a little misshapen dwarf, who pattered after her with ridiculous movements which always made me laugh. Night after night, during a certain year of my life, this pantomime never failed to follow the extinguishment of the candle, and it was to me a never-failing source of delight.

One thing was peculiar about these forms—they appeared to cause a vibration of the great central nerves of the body, as when a harp-string is struck. So, I could feel in myself the jar of the dwarf's pattering feet, the soft, rhythmic movement of the little woman stroking down her long hair, the vibrations of the violin, and the steps of the dancing old woman. Nobody knew of this still and hidden world of pleasure which was thus nightly open to me. My mother used often to wonder, when, hours after she put me to bed, she would find me lying perfectly quiet, with my eyes widely and calmly open. Once or twice I undertook to tell her what I saw, but was hushed up with, "Nonsense, child! there hasn't been anybody in the room; you shouldn't talk so."

The one thing that was held above all things sacred and inviolable in a child's education in those old Puritan days was to form habits of truth. Every statement received an immediate and unceremonious sifting, and anything that looked in the least like a departure from actual verity was met with prompt and stringent discouragement. When my mother repeated before Aunt Lois some of my strange sayings, she was met with the downright declaration: "That child will be an awful liar, Susy, if you don't keep a strict lookout on him. Don't you let him tell you any stories like that."

So, I early learned silence; but my own confidence in the reality of my secondary world was not a whit diminished. Like Galileo, who said, "It does move, nevertheless," so I, when I once had the candle out at night, snapped my fingers mentally at Aunt Lois, and enjoyed my vision.

One peculiarity of these appearances was that certain of them seemed like a sort of *genii loci*—shapes belonging to certain places. The apparition of the fairy woman with the golden girdle only appeared in a certain room where I slept one year, and which had across one of its corners a sort of closet called a buffet. From this buffet the vision took its rise, and when my parents moved to another house it never appeared again.

A similar event in my shadow-world had marked our coming to my grandmother's to live. The old violin-player and his wife had for a long time been my nightly entertainers; but the first night after we were established in the apartment given up to our use by Aunt Lois, I saw them enter as they usually did, seeming to come right through the wall of the room. They, however, surveyed the apartment with a sort of confused, discontented movement, and seemed to talk to each other with their backs to me; finally, I heard the old woman say, "We can't stay here," and immediately I saw them passing through the wall of the house. I saw after them as clearly as if the wall had dissolved and given my eyes the vision of all out of doors. They went to my grandfather's wood-pile and looked irresolutely round; finally, they mounted on the pile, and seemed to sink gradually through it and disappear, and I never saw them afterwards.

But another of the companions of my solitude was more constant to me. This was the form of a young boy of about my own age, who for a year past had frequently come to me at night, and seemed to look lovingly upon me, and with whom

I used to have a sort of social communion, without words, in a manner which seemed to me far more perfect than human language. I thought to him, and in return I received silent demonstrations of sympathy and fellowship from him. I called him Harvey, and used, as I lay looking in his face, mentally to tell him many things about the books I read, the games I played, and the childish joys and griefs I had; and in return he seemed to express affection and sympathy by a strange communication, as lovers sometimes talk to each other by distant glances.

Attendant on all these exceptional experiences, perhaps resulting from them, was a peculiar manner of viewing the human beings by whom I was surrounded. It is common now-a-days to speak of the sphere or emanation that surrounds a person. To my childish mind there was a vivid perception of something of this nature with regard to everyone whom I approached. There were people for whom I had a violent and instinctive aversion, whose presence in the room gave me a pain so positive that it seemed almost physical, and others, again, to whom I was strongly attracted, and whose presence near me filled me with agreeable sensations, of which I could give no very definite account.

For this reason, I suppose, the judgments which different people formed concerning me varied extremely. Miss Mehitable, for example, by whom I was strongly attracted, thought me one of the most amiable of boys; while my poor Aunt Lois was certain I was one of the most trying children that ever were born.

My poor mother! I surely loved her, and yet her deficient vital force, her continual sadness and discouragement, acted on my nerves as a constant weight and distress, against which I blindly and instinctively struggled; while Aunt Lois's very footstep on the stair seemed to rouse every nerve of combativeness in my little body into a state of bristling tension. I remember that when I was about six or seven years old, I had the scarlet fever, and Aunt Lois, who was a most rampant and energetic sick-nurse, undertook to watch with me; but my cries and resistance were so terrible that I was thought to be going deranged.

Finally, the matter was adjusted by Sam Lawson's offering to take the place, upon which I became perfectly tranquil, and resigned myself into his hands with the greatest composure and decorum. Sam was to me, during my childhood, a guide, philosopher, and friend. The lazy, easy, indefinite atmosphere of being that surrounded him was to me like the haze of Indian summer over a landscape, and I delighted to bask in it. Nothing about him was any more fixed than the wavering shadows of clouds; he was a boundless world of narrative and dreamy suggestion, tending to no point and having no end, and in it I delighted.

Sam, besides, had a partiality for all those haunts in which I took pleasure. Near our house was the old town burying-ground, where reposed the bones of generations of Indian *sachems*, elders, pastors, and teachers, converted from the wild forests, who, Christianised and churched, died in the faith, and were gathered into Christian burial. On its green hillocks I loved to sit and watch and dream long after sundown or moonrise, and fancy I saw bands of wavering shapes, and hope that someone out of the crowd might have a smile of recognition or a spiritual word for me.

My mother and grandmother and Aunt Lois were horror-stricken by such propensities, indicating neither more nor less than indefinite coughs and colds, with early death in the rear; and however much in the way a little boy always seemed in those times in the active paths of his elders, yet it was still esteemed a primary duty to keep him in the world. "Horace, what do you go and sit in the graveyard for?" would my grandmother say. "I should think you'd be 'fraid something would 'pear to you."

"I want something to appear, grandmother."

"Pshaw, pshaw! no, you don't. What do you want to be so odd for? Don't you ever say such things."

Sam, however, was willing to aid and abet me in strolling and lounging anywhere and at any hour, and lent a willing ear to my tales of what I saw, and had in his capacious wallet a pendent story or a spiritual precedent for anything that I could mention.

On this night, after he had left me, I went to bed with my mind full of the haunted house, and all that was to be hoped or feared from its exploration. Whether this was the cause or not, the result was that Harvey appeared nearer and more friendly than ever; and he held by his hand another boy, whose figure appeared to me like a faintly discerned form in a mist. Sometimes the mist seemed to waver and part, and I caught indistinct glimpses of bright yellow curls and clear blue eyes, and then Harvey smiled and shook his head. When he began to disappear, he said to me, "Goodbye"; and I felt an inward assurance that he was about to leave me. I said my "Goodbye" aloud, and stretched out my hands.

"Why, Horace, Horace!" said my mother, waking suddenly at the sound of my voice—"Horace, wake up; you've been dreaming."

I had not even been asleep, but I did not tell her so, and turning over, as I usually did when the curtain fell over my dreamland, I was soon asleep. I was wide awake with the earliest peep of dawn the next morning, and had finished dressing myself before my mother awoke.

Ours was an early household, and the brisk tap of Aunt Lois's footsteps, and the rattling of chairs and dishes in the kitchen, showed that breakfast was in active preparation.

My grandfather's prediction with regard to my Uncle Eliakim proved only too correct. The fact was, that the poor man lived always in the whirl of a perfect Maelstrom of promises and engagements, which were constantly converging towards every hour of his unoccupied time. His old wagon and horse both felt the effects of such incessant activity, and such deficient care and attention as were consequent upon it, and were at all times in a state of dilapidation. Therefore, it was that the next morning nine, ten, and eleven o'clock appeared, and no Uncle Eliakim.

Sam Lawson had for more than two hours been seated in an expectant attitude on our doorstep; but as the sun shone warm, and he had a large mug of cider between his hands, he appeared to enjoy his mind with great equanimity.

Aunt Lois moved about the house with an air and manner of sharp contempt, which exhibited itself even in the way she did her household tasks. She put down plates as if she despised them, and laid sticks of wood on the fire with defiant thumps, as much as to say that she knew some things that had got to be in time and place if others were not but she spake no word.

Aunt Lois, as I have often said before, was a good Christian, and held it her duty to govern her tongue. True, she said many sharp and bitter things; but nobody but herself and her God knew how many more she would have said had she not reined herself up in conscientious silence. But never was there a woman whose silence could express more contempt and displeasure than hers. You could feel it in the air about you, though she never said a word. You could feel it in the rustle of her dress, in the tap of her heels over the floor, in the occasional flash of her sharp, black eye. She was like a thunder-cloud whose quiet is portentous, and from which you every moment expect a flash or an explosion. This whole morning's excursion was contrary to her mind and judgment—an ill-advised, ill-judged, shiftless proceeding, and being entered on in a way as shiftless.

"What time do you suppose it is, mother?" she at last said to my grandmother, who was busy in her buttery.

"Massy, Lois! I daren't look," called out my grandmother who was apt to fall behindhand of her desires in the amount of work she could bring to pass of a morning. "I don't want to know."

"Well, it's eleven o'clock," said Lois, relentlessly, "and no signs of Uncle 'Liakim yet; and there's Sam Lawson, I s'pose he's going to spend the day on our doorstep."

Sam Lawson looked after my Aunt Lois as she went out of the kitchen. "Lordy massy, Horace, I wouldn't be so kind o' unreconciled as she is all the time for nothin'. Now *I* might get into a fluster 'cause *I*'m kep' a waitin', but I don't. I think it's our duty to be willin' to wait quiet till things come round; this 'ere's a world where things can't be driv', and folks mustn't set their heart on havin' everything come out jes' so, 'cause ef they do the'll allers be in a stew, like Hepsy and Miss Lois there. Let 'em jest wait quiet, and things allers do come round in the and as well or better 'n ef you worried."

And as if to illustrate and justify this train of thought, Uncle Eliakim's wagon at this moment came round the corner of the street, driving at a distracted pace. The good man came with such headlong speed and vivacity that his straw hat was taken off by the breeze, and flew far behind him, and he shot up to our door, as he usually did to that of the meeting-house, as if he were going to drive straight in.

"Lordy massy, Mr. Sheril," said Sam, "don't get out; I'll get your hat. Horace, you jest run and pick it up; that's a good boy."

I ran accordingly, but my uncle had sprung out as lively as an autumn grasshopper. "I've been through a sea of troubles this morning," he said. "I lent my waggin to Jake Marshall yesterday afternoon, to take his wife a ride. I thought if Jake was a mind to pay the poor woman any attention, I'd help; but when he brought it back last night, one of the bolts was broken, and the harness gave out in two places."

"Want to know?" said Sam, leisurely examining the establishment. "I think the neighbours ought to subscribe to keep up your team, Mr. Sheril, for it's free to the hull on 'em."

"And what thanks does he get?" said Aunt Lois, sharply. "Well, Uncle 'Liakim, it's almost dinner-time."

"I know it, I know it, I know it, Lois. But there's been a lot o' things to do this morning. Just as I got the waggin mended come Aunt Bathsheba Sawin's boy and put me in mind that I promised to carry her corn to grind; and I had to stop and take that round to mill; and then I remembered the pills that was to go to Hannah Dexter—"

"I dare say, and forty more things like it," said Aunt Lois.

"Well, jump in now," said Uncle Fly; "we'll be over and back in no time."

"You may as well put it off till after dinner now," said Aunt Lois.

"Couldn't stop for that," said Uncle 'Liakim; "my afternoon Is all full now. I've got to be in twenty places before night" And away we rattled, while Aunt Lois stood looking after us in silent, unutterable contempt.

"Stop! Stop! Stop! Whoa! Whoa!" said Uncle 'Liakim, drawing suddenly up. "There's that plaster for Widdah Peters, after all. I wonder if Lois wouldn't just run up with it." By this time he had turned the horse, who ran, with his usual straightforward, blind directness, in a right line, against the a doorstep again.

"Well, what now?" said Aunt Lois, appearing at the door,

"Why, Lois, I've just come back to tell you I forgot I promised to carry Widdah Peters that plaster for lumbago; couldn't you just find time to run up there with it?"

"Well, give it to me," said Aunt Lois, with sharp precision, and an air of desperate patience.

"Yes, yes, I will," said Uncle Fly, standing up and beginning a rapid search into that series of pockets which form a distinguishing mark of masculine habiliments—searching with such hurried zeal that he really seemed intent on tearing himself to pieces. "Here 't is!—no, pshaw, pshaw! That's my handkerchief! O, here!—pshaw, pshaw! Why, where is it? Didn't I put it in?—or did I—O, here it is in my vest-pocket; no; though. Where a plague!" and Uncle Fly sprang from the wagon and began his usual active round-and-round chase after himself, slapping his pockets, now before and now behind, and whirling like a dancing *dervis*, while Aunt Lois stood regarding him with stony composure.

"If you *could* ever think where anything was, before you began to talk about it, it would be an improvement," she said.

"Well, fact is," said Uncle Eliakim, "now I think of it, Mis' Sheril made me change my coat just as I came out, and that's the whole on't. You just run up, Lois, and tell Mis' Sheril to send one of the boys down to Widdah Peters's with the plaster she'll find in the pocket—right-hand side. Come now, get up.

These last words were addressed, not to Aunt Lois, but to the horse, who, kept in rather a hungry and craving state by his master's hurrying manner of life, had formed the habit of sedulously improving every spare interval in catching at a mouthful of anything to eat, and had been accordingly busy in cropping away a fringe of very green grass that was growing up by the kitchen doorstep, from which occupation he was remorselessly twitched up and started on an impetuous canter.

"Wal, now I hope we're fairly started," said Sam Lawson; "and, Mr. Sheril, you may as well, while you are about it, take the right road as the wrong one, 'cause that 'ere saves time. It pleasant enough anywhere, to be sure, today; but when a body goin' to a place, a body likes to get there, as it were."

"Well, well, well," said Uncle Fly, "we're on the right road, ain't we?"

"Wal, so fur you be; but when you come out on the plains, you must take the fust left-hand road that drives through the woods, and you may jest as well know as much aforehand."

"Much obliged to you," said my uncle. "I reely hadn't thought particularly about the way."

"S'pose not," said Sam, composedly; "so it's jest as well you took me along. Lordy massy, there ain't a road nor a cart-path round Old town that I hain't been over, time and time agin. I believe I could get through any on 'em the darkest night that ever was hatched. Jake Marshall and me has been Indianing round these 'ere woods more times 'n you could count. It's kind o' pleasant, a nice bright day like this 'ere, to be a joggin' along in the woods. Everything so sort o' still, ye know; and ye hear the chestnuts a droppin', and the walnuts. Jake and me, last fall, went up by Widdah Peters's one day, and shuck them trees, and got nigh about a good bushel o' wa'nuts. I used to kind o' like to crack 'em for the young uns, nights, last winter, when Hepsy'd let 'em sit up. Though she's allers for drivin' on 'em all off to bed, and makin' it kind o' solitary, Hepsy is." And Sam concluded the conjugal allusion with a deep sigh.

"Have you ever been into the grounds of the Dench house?" said Uncle Fly.

"Wal, no, not reely; but Jake, he has; and ben into the house too. There was a fellow named 'Biah Smith that used to be a kind o' servant to the next family that come in after Lady Frankland went out, and he took Jake all over it once when there wa'n't nobody there. 'Biah, he said that when Sir Harry lived there, there was one room that was always kept shet up, and wa'n't never gone into, and in that 'ere room there was the long red cloak, and the hat and sword, and all the clothes he hed on when he was buried under the ruins in that 'ere earthquake. They said that every year, when the day of the earthquake come round, Sir Harry used to spend It a fastin' and prayin' in that 'ere room, all alone. 'Biah says that he had talked with a fellow that was one of

Sir Harry's body-servants, and he told him that Sir Harry used to come out o' that 'ere room lookin' more like a ghost than a live man, when he'd fasted and prayed for twenty-four hours there. Nobody knows what might have 'peared to him there."

I wondered much in my own quiet way at this story, and marvelled whether, in Sir Harry's long, penitential watchings, he had seen the air of the room all tremulous with forms and faces such as glided around me in my solitary hours.

"Naow, you see," said Sam Lawson, "when the earthquake come, Sir Harry, he was a driving with a court lady; and she, poor soul, went into 'tarnity in a minit,—'thout a minit to prepare. And I 'spect there ain't no reason to s'pose but what she was a poor, mis'able Roman Catholic. So, her prospects couldn't have been noways encouragin'. And it must have borne on Sir Harry's mind to think she should be took and he spared, when he was a cuttin' up just in the way he was. I shouldn't wonder but she should 'pear to him. You know they say there is a woman in white walks them grounds, and 'Biah, he says, as near as he can find out, it's that 'ere particular chamber as she allers goes to. 'Biah said he'd seen her at the windows a wringin' her hands and a cryin' fit to break her heart, poor soul. Kind o' makes a body feel bad, 'cause, arter all, 't wa'n't her fault she was born a Roman Catholic—now was it?"

The peculiarity of my own mental history had this effect on me from a child, that it wholly took away from me all dread of the supernatural. A world of shadowy forms had always been as much a part of my short earthly experience as the more solid and tangible one of real people. I had just as quiet and natural a feeling about one as the other. I had not the slightest doubt, on hearing Sam's story, that the form of the white lady did tenant those deserted apartments; and so far from feeling any chill or dread in the idea, I felt only a sort of curiosity to make her acquaintance.

Our way to the place wound through miles of dense forest Sir Harry had chosen it, as a retreat from the prying eyes and slanderous tongues of the world, in a region of woodland solitude. And as we trotted leisurely under the bright scarlet and yellow boughs of the forest, Uncle Eliakim and Sam discoursed of the traditions of the place we were going to.

"Who was it bought the place after Lady Frankland went to England?" said Uncle Eliakim.

"Wal, I believe 'twas let a spell. There was some French folks hed it 'long through the war. I heerd tell that they was pretty high people. I never could quite make out when they went off; there was a good many stories round about it. I didn't clearly make out how 'twas, till Dench got it. Dench, you know, got his money in a pretty peculiar way, ef all they says's true."

"How's that?" said my uncle.

"Wal, they do say he got the great carbuncle that was at the bottom of Sepaug River. You've heard about the great carbuncle, I s'pose?"

"O, no! do pray tell me about it," said I, interrupting with fervour.

"Why, didn't you never hear 'bout that? want to know. Wal, I'l tell ye, then. I know all 'bout it. Jake Marshall, he told me that Dench fust told him, and he got it from old Mother Ketury, ye know,—a regelar old heathen Injun Ketury is—and folks do go so fur as to say that in the old times Ketury'd 'a' ben took up for a witch, though I never see no harm in her ways. Ef there be sperits, and we all know there is, what's the harm o' Ketury's seein' on 'em?"

"Maybe she can't help seeing them," suggested I.

"Jes' so, jes' so; that 'ere's what I telled Jake when we's a talkin' it over, and he said he didn't like Dench's havin' so much to do with old Ketury. But la, old Ketury could say the Lord's Prayer in Injun, 'cause I've heard her; though she wouldn't say it when she didn't want to and she would say it when she did—jest as the fit took her. But lordy massy, them wild Injuns, they ain't but jest half folks, they're so kind o' wild, and birchy and busby as a body may say. Ef they lake religion at all it's got to be in their own way. Ef you get the wild beast all out o' one on 'em, there don't somehow seem to be enough left to make an ordinary smart man of, so much on 'em's wild. Anyhow, Dench, he was thick with Ketury, and she told him all about the gret carbuncle, and gin him directions how to get it."

"But I don't know what a great carbuncle is," I interrupted.

"Lordy massy, boy, didn't you never read in your Bible about the New Jerusalem, and the precious stones in the foundation, that shone like the sun? Wal, the carbuncle was one on 'em."

"Did it fall down out of heaven into the river?" said I.

"Mebbe," said Sam. "At any rate Ketury, she told 'em what they had to do to get it They had to go out arter it jest exactly at twelve o'clock at night, when the moon was full. You was to fast all the day before, and go fastin', and say the Lord's Prayer in Injun afore you went; and when you come to where 'twas, you was to dive after it. But there wa'n't to be a word spoke; if there was, it went right off."

"What did they have to say the prayer in Indian for?" said I.

"Lordy massy, boy, I s'pose 'twas 'cause 'twas Indian sperits kep' a watch over it. Any rate 'twas considerable of a pull on 'em, 'cause Ketury, she had to teach 'em; and she wa'n't allers in the sperit on't Sometimes she's crosser 'n torment, Ketury is. Dench, he gin her fust and last as much as ten dollars—so Jake says. However, they got all through with it, and then come a moonlight night, and they went out. Jake says it was the splendidest moonlight ye ever did see,—all jest as still,—only the frogs and the turtles kind o' peepin'; and they didn't say a word, and rowed out past the pint there, where the water's ten feet deep, and he looked down and see it a shinin' on the bottom like a great star, making the waters all light like a lantern.

"Dench, he dived for it, Jake said; and he saw him put his hand right on it; and he was so tickled, you know, to see he'd got it, that he couldn't help hollerin' right out, 'There, you got it!' and it was gone. Dench was mad enough to 'a' killed him 'cause, when it goes that 'ere way, you can't see it agin for a year and a day. But two or three years arter, all of a sudden Dench, he seemed to kind o' spruce up and have a deal o' money to spend. He said an uncle had died and left it to him in England; but Jake Marshall says you'll never take him in that 'ere way. He says he thinks it's no better 'n witchcraft, getting money that 'ere way. Ye see Jake was to have had half if they'd 'a' got it, and not gettin' nothin' kind o' sot him to thinkin' on it in a moral pint o' view, ye know.—But, lordy massy, where be we, Mr. Sheril? This 'ere's the second or third time we've come round to this 'ere old dead chestnut. We ain't makin' no progress."

In fact there were many and crossing cart-paths through this forest, which had been worn by different farmers of the vicinity in going after their yearly supply of wood; and, notwithstanding Sam's assertion of superior knowledge in these matters, we had, in the negligent inattention of his narrative, become involved in this labyrinth, and driven up and down, and back and forward, in the wood, without seeming at all to advance upon our errand.

"Wal, I declare for't, I never did see nothing beat it," said Sam. "We've been goin' jest round and round for this hour or more, and come out again at exactly the same place. I've heerd of places that's kep' hid, and folks allers gets sort o' struck blind and confused that undertakes to look 'em up. Wal, I don't say I believe in sich stories, but this 'ere is curous. Why, I'd 'a' thought I could 'a' gone straight to it blindfolded, any day. Ef Jake Marshall was here, he'd go straight to it."

"Well, Sam," said Uncle Eliakim, "it's maybe because you and me got so interested in telling stories that we've missed the way."

"That 'ere's it, 'thout a doubt," said Sam. "Now I'll jist hush up, and kind o' concentrate my 'tention. I'll just git out and walk a spell, and take an observation."

The result of this improved attention to the material facts of the case was, that we soon fell into a road that seemed to wind slowly up a tract of rising ground, and to disclose to our view, through an interlacing of distant boughs, the western horizon, toward which the sun was now sinking with long, level beams. We had been such a time in our wanderings, that there seemed a prospect of night setting in before we should be through with our errand and ready to return.

"The house stands on the top of a sort o' swell o' ground," said Sam; "and as nigh as I can make it out, it must be somewhere about there."

"There is a woman a little way before us," said I; "why don't you ask her?"

I saw very plainly in a turn of the road a woman whose face was hidden by a bonnet, who stood as if waiting for us. It was not the white woman of ghostly memory, but apparently a veritable person in the everyday habiliments of common life, who stood as if waiting for us.

"I don't see no woman," said Sam; "where is she?"

I pointed with my finger, but as I did so the form melted away. I remember distinctly the leaves of the trees back of it appearing through it as through a gauze veil, and then it disappeared entirely.

"There isn't any woman that I can see," said Uncle Eliakim, briskly. "The afternoon sun must have got into your eyes, boy."

I had been so often severely checked and reproved for stating what I saw, that I now determined to keep silence, whatever might appear to me. At a little distance before us the road forked, one path being steep and craggy, and the other easier of ascent, and apparently going in much the same general direction. A little in advance, in the more rugged path, stood the same female form. Her face was hidden by a branch of a tree, but she beckoned to us. "Take *that* path. Uncle 'Liakim," said I, it's the right one."

"Lordy massy," said Sam Lawson, "how in the world should you know that? That 'ere is the shortest road to the Dench Souse, and the other leads away from it."

I kept silence as to my source of information, and still watched the figure. As we passed it, I saw a beautiful face with a serene and tender expression, and her hands were raised as if in blessing. I looked back earnestly and she was gone.

A few moments after, we were in the grounds of the place, and struck into what had formerly been the carriage way, though now overgrown with weeds, and here and there with a jungle of what was once well-kept ornamental shrubbery. A tree had been uprooted by the late tempest, and blown down across the road, and we had to make quite a little detour to avoid it.

"Now how are we to get into this house?" said Uncle Eliakim. "No doubt it's left fastened up."

"Do you see *that?*" said Sam Lawson, who had been gazing steadily upward at the chimneys of the house, with his eyes shaded by one of his great hands. "Look at that smoke from the middle chimbly."

"There's somebody in the house, to be sure," said Uncle Eliakim; "suppose we knock at the front door here?"—and with great briskness, suiting the action to the word, he lifted the black serpent knocker, and gave such a *rat tat tat* as must have roused all the echoes of the old house, while Sam Lawson and I stood by him, expectant, on the front steps.

Sam then seated himself composedly on a sort of bench which was placed under the shadow of the porch, and awaited the result with the contentment of a man of infinite leisure. Uncle Eliakim, however, felt pressed for time, and therefore gave another long and vehement rap. Very soon a chirping of childish voices was heard behind the door, and a pattering of feet; there appeared to be a sort of consultation.

"There they be now," said Sam Lawson, "jest as I told you."

"Please go round to the back door," said a childish voice; "this is locked, and I can't open it."

We all immediately followed Sam Lawson, who took enormous strides over the shrubbery, and soon I saw the vision of a curly-headed, blue-eyed boy holding open the side door of the house.

I ran up to him. "Are you Harvey?" I said.

"No," he answered; "my name isn't Harvey, it's Harry; and this is my sister Tina,"—and immediately a pair of dark eyes looked out over his shoulder.

"Well, we've come to take you to my grandmother's house," said I.

I don't know how it was, but I always spoke of our domestic establishment under the style and title of the female ruler. It was grandmother's house.

"I am glad of it," said the boy, "for we have tried two or three times to find our way to Oldtown, and got lost in the woods and had to come back here again."

Here the female partner in the concern stepped a little forward, eager for her share in the conversation. "Do you know old

Sol?" she said.

"Lordy massy, I do," said Sam Lawson, quite delighted at this verification of the identity of the children. "Yes, I see him only day afore yesterday, and he was 'quirin' arter you, and we thought we'd find you over in this 'ere house, 'cause I'd seen smoke a comin' out o' the chimblies. Had a putty good time in the old house, I reckon. Ben all over it pretty much, hain't ye?"

"O yes," said Tina; "and it's such a strange old place—a great big house with ever so many rooms in it!"

"Wal, we'll jest go over it, being as we're here," said Sam; and into it we all went.

Now there was nothing in the world that little Miss Tina took more native delight in than in playing the hostess. To entertain was her dearest instinct, and she hastened with all speed to open before us all in the old mansion that her own rummaging and investigating talents had brought to light, chattering meanwhile with the spirit of a bobolink.

"You don't know," she said to Sam Lawson, "what a curious little closet there is in here, with bookcases and drawers, and a looking-glass in the door, with a curtain over it."

"Want to know?" said Sam. "Wal, that 'ere does beat all. It's some of them old English folks's grander, I s'pose."

"And here's a picture of such a beautiful lady, that always looks at you, whichever way you go,—just see."

"Lordy massy, so 't does. Wal, now, them drawers, mebbe, have got curious things in 'em," suggested Sam.

"O yes, but Harry never would let me look in them. I tried, though, once, when Harry was gone; but, if you'll believe me, they're all locked."

"Want to know?" said Sam. "That 'ere's a kind o' pity now."

"Would *you* open them? You wouldn't, would you?" said the little one, turning suddenly round and opening her great wide eyes full on him. "Harry said the place wasn't ours, and It wouldn't be proper."

"Wal, he's a nice boy; quite right in him. Little folks mustn't touch things that ain't theirn," said Sam, who was strong on the moralities; though, after all, when all the rest had left the apartment, I looked back and saw him giving a sly tweak to the drawers of the cabinet on his own individual account.

"I was just a makin' sure, you know, that 'twas all safe," he said, as he caught my eye, and saw that he was discovered.

Sam revelled and expatiated, however, in the information that lay before him in the exploration of the house. No tourist with Murray's guide-book in hand, and with travels to prepare for publication, ever went more patiently through the doing of a place. Not a door was left closed that could be opened; not a passage unexplored. Sam's head came out dusty and cobwebby between the beams of the ghostly old garret, where mouldy relics of antique furniture were reposing, and disappeared into the gloom of the spacious cellars, where the light was as darkness. He found none of the marks of the traditional haunted room; but he prolonged the search till there seemed a prospect that poor Uncle Eliakim would have to get him away by physical force, if we meant to get home in time for supper.

"Mr. Lawson, you don't seem to remember we haven't any of us had a morsel of dinner, and the sun is actually going down. The folks'll be concerned about us. Come, let's take the children and be off."

And so we mounted briskly into the wagon, and the old horse, vividly impressed with the idea of barn and hay at the end of his toils, seconded the vigorous exertions of Uncle Fly, and we rattled and spun on our homeward career, and arrived at the farmhouse a little after moonrise.

LEONAUR

ALSO FROM LEONAUR
AVAILABLE IN SOFTCOVER OR HARDCOVER WITH DUST JACKET

MR MUKERJI'S GHOSTS *by S. Mukerji*—Supernatural tales from the British Raj period by India's Ghost story collector.

KIPLINGS GHOSTS *by Rudyard Kipling*—Twelve stories of Ghosts, Hauntings, Curses, Werewolves & Magic.

THE COLLECTED SUPERNATURAL AND WEIRD FICTION OF WASHINGTON IRVING: VOLUME 1 *by Washington Irving*—Including one novel 'A History of New York', and nine short stories of the Strange and Unusual.

THE COLLECTED SUPERNATURAL AND WEIRD FICTION OF WASHINGTON IRVING: VOLUME 2 *by Washington Irving*—Including three novelettes 'The Legend of the Sleepy Hollow', 'Dolph Heyliger', 'The Adventure of the Black Fisherman' and thirty-two short stories of the Strange and Unusual.

THE COLLECTED SUPERNATURAL AND WEIRD FICTION OF JOHN KENDRICK BANGS: VOLUME 1 *by John Kendrick Bangs*—Including one novel 'Toppleton's Client or A Spirit in Exile', and ten short stories of the Strange and Unusual.

THE COLLECTED SUPERNATURAL AND WEIRD FICTION OF JOHN KENDRICK BANGS: VOLUME 2 *by John Kendrick Bangs*—Including four novellas 'A House-Boat on the Styx', 'The Pursuit of the House-Boat', 'The Enchanted Typewriter' and 'Mr. Munchausen' of the Strange and Unusual.

THE COLLECTED SUPERNATURAL AND WEIRD FICTION OF JOHN KENDRICK BANGS: VOLUME 3 *by John Kendrick Bangs*—Including twor novellas 'Olympian Nights', 'Roger Camerden: A Strange Story', and ten short stories of the Strange and Unusual.

THE COLLECTED SUPERNATURAL AND WEIRD FICTION OF MARY SHELLEY: VOLUME 1 *by Mary Shelley*—Including one novel 'Frankenstein or the Modern Prometheus', and fourteen short stories of the Strange and Unusual.

THE COLLECTED SUPERNATURAL AND WEIRD FICTION OF MARY SHELLEY: VOLUME 2 *by Mary Shelley*—Including one novel 'The Last Man', and three short stories of the Strange and Unusual.

THE COLLECTED SUPERNATURAL AND WEIRD FICTION OF AMELIA B. EDWARDS *by Amelia B. Edwards*—Contains two novelettes 'Monsieur Maurice', and 'The Discovery of the Treasure Isles', one ballad 'A Legend of Boisguilbert'and seventeen short stories to cill the blood.